I0625896

MERLIN AND THE KILLER CRUSH

WYLD ENCHANTMENT WOODS
COZY MYSTERY

Kura Jane Carpenter

WUP

Wicked Unicorn Press

Published by **Wicked Unicorn Press**

National Library of New Zealand Cataloguing-in-Publication Data
Merlin and the Killer Crush / Kura Jane Carpenter
softcover ISBN 978-1-0670080-0-0

Map of Ella's Home

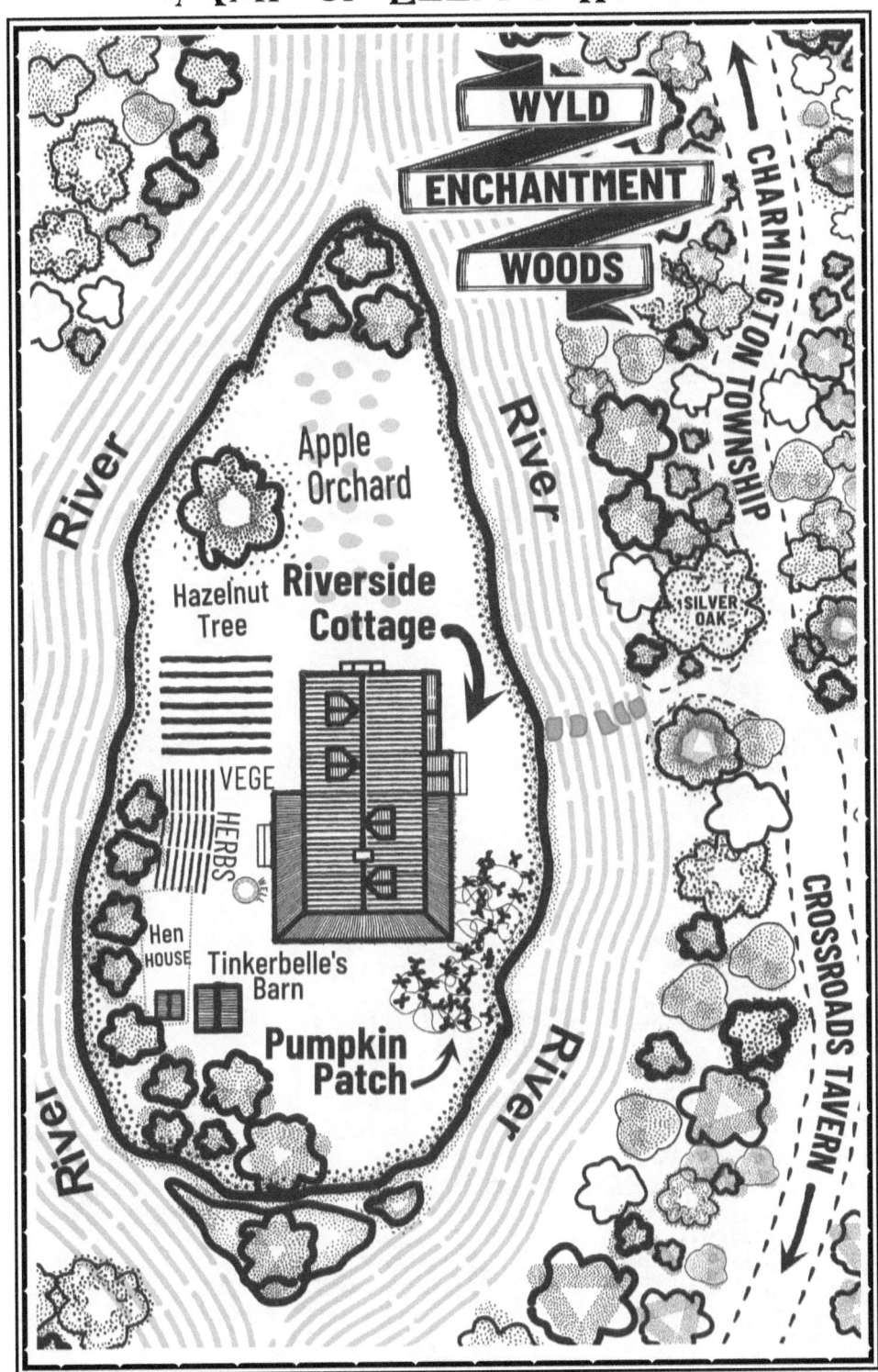

CHARMINGTON TO NOTTINGHAM

CONTENTS

Cast of Characters VI
Ella's Lesson Plan 1
Merlin Heckles Doctor Hyde 8
The Crush 13
Lessons Learned 18
Rogues 27
Observations and Conjecture 34
What the Midwife Saw 37
Avalon Books and Stationery 42
Cinderella puts Claude on the Spot 47
The Clue in the Name 51
The Queen's Conundrum 54
Prince John's Plan 58
The Mayor's Luncheon turns Deadly 61
Merlin's Secret 67
The Huntsman Tavern gets an Upgrade 70
What the Letter Said 74
Wulf 78
The Cinderella Memorial Park Snow Fight 83
Cutthroat Gwen 89
Hiding in Plain Sight 91
The Handsome Mystery Stranger Revealed 96
The Astute 100
The Test Results 105
Tom Cries Foul while Merlin Bewitches 110
Magic Touch Day Spa 114
Marley's Office and the Messenger 118
All the World's a Stage 122
The Secret Behind the Feud Revealed 125
Sally's Last Chance 128
The Flying Carpet 137
The Final Showdown 142
Home Again Home Again 146
Next in Series... 149
Acknowledgements 150
About the Author 150

Cast of Characters

- **Ella Charming** – Twin sister of Sibylla, sibling of Merlin, Arabella, and Cinderella.
- **Tom April** – Rookie Castle Guardsman - Accidentally swapped bodies with Ella's cat Tilly.
- Axel Luther – Charmington Sheriff - Former Capt. of the Castle guards.
- Bethany – Child – Great Granddaughter of Betty.
- Betty – Pie shop Owner.
- Mr. Beau – Shoeshiner and Lamp Lighter.
- Bron the Baker – Proprietor of Southgate Bakery.
- Cassidy Turpin – Night watch Guardswoman – Niece of Dirk.
- Cheapcuts / Chelton Junior – Son of Martha and Chelton.
- Chelton – Butcher – Husband of Martha.
- Cinderella (deceased) – Princess – Sister of Ella and Sibylla.
- Claude – Bookstore Owner – Originally an Actor from Avalon.
- Cole – Handyman.
- Dirk Turpin – Royal coachman – Uncle of Cassidy Turpin.
- Doctor Edison Hyde – Doctor of Hot Cockle Lane Hospital.
- Mistress Fairweather – Matron of the Baker Street orphanage.
- Goldilocks – Royal hairdresser and Magical Healer.
- Gretel – Vampire – Stage Coach & Tavern owner – Sister of Hansel.
- Gwen Pendragon – Merlin's Publisher.
- Hansel – Vampire – Stage Coach & Tavern owner – Brother of Gretel.
- Harold Harper – Postmaster.
- Mrs. Haversham – Former headmistress of the Haversham Academy.
- Katie – Clerk at the Police Station.
- Marge – Midwife – A notorious gossip.
- Martha Chelton – Wife of Chelton the butcher.
- Merlin – Famous Magician – Brother to Ella & Sibylla.
- Millie Mercer – Haberdashery owner – Twin sister of Sally.
- Olly May – Sally's young ward.
- Mr. Puddles – Willow's pet poodle.
- Nigella Pickford – Actress – Director of Pickford Players.
- Prince John – Regent of Sherwood.
- Mr. Rat – Sam's pet rat.
- Richard – Woodcutter – Husband of Cinderella.
- Robinne Scarlett – Brewer at the Crossroads Tavern.
- Sally Mercer – Haberdashery owner – Twin sister of Millie.
- Sandy and Sam – Baker Street Orphan children.
- Sebastian – Mayor of Charmington – Grandfather of Spalding.
- Sibylla – Queen of Wyld Kingdom – Twin sister of Ella.
- Sisters Grimm – Alleged Authors of the popular novel *Cinderella*.
- Spalding – Actor – Grandson of the Mayor.
- Tobias – Schoolmaster – Aspiring romance novelist.
- Willow – Baker and Herbalist Witch.
- Wulf – Bodyguard to Prince John.

CHAPTER 1

ELLA'S LESSON PLAN

TAX OFFICE, TOWN HALL ATTIC, NORTHGATE SQUARE, CHARMINGTON.

"Qwerty? The keys aren't in alphabetical order?" Ella Charming eyed the heavy black typewriter on a desk in the Charmington Tax office. The device's gleaming rows of letters loomed like hungry teeth waiting to snap. She stood and peered at the other typewriters scattered about the large attic space. "This machine must be a dud."

"Relax, it's not a dud. Sit back down." Perched on the desk in front of her, Tomcat grinned, flashing its own set of sharp pearly canines. Three months ago Ella's fluffy white cat Tilly had switched bodies with a young town guard, Tom April, in a magical accident. "It's not like you to be nervous. C'mon now," Tomcat coaxed. "Take your seat and quit stalling."

Ella thinned her lips. "Wasn't stalling," she fibbed and slumped back down into the chair.

Tomcat tapped the new-fangled contraption. "Put the clean sheet of paper between these rollers, and then wind this knob. It feeds the paper right into the body of the mechanism."

Cautiously, Ella turned the knob, pulling the sheet of paper into the typewriter at each click of the wheel. "So far, so good. Wherever did you learn to use a typewriter?"

Early morning wintery light filtered across the quiet room as Tomcat sat back. "The bigger question is, how come you haven't? Too busy attending balls and turning pumpkins into carriages? Come on, Your Highness. Next step, the keyboard. Have you got your lesson plan handy?"

Ella regarded her notes, handwritten the night before, that she had planned to copy out. She squinted at the first line *'There are four states of wyld magic'* and then back at the keyboard to locate the letter T. "Aha, there it is! Tee." She pressed the bright shiny key with a bony index finger. A lever within the typewriter flopped out and hit the paper with a satisfying *whap*.

"Good!" praised Tomcat, peering at the inky black letter now fresh on the paper. "Keep hitting the keys like that, with a good firm press. You're doing great."

Ella rocked back in her chair, her nerves ebbing. "That was rather fun! Now, where's the H?" She trailed her index finger across the little round keys until she located it and gave it a solid tap. "Aha! Take that! No one said how pleasant striking the keys would feel! Now, where's the E?"

Tomcat's paw darted in front of her face and pointed to the E, which Ella struck with a quick snap. "Lost my place now," she muttered, glancing back at the looping cursive of her handwriting. "Maybe you could read out my lesson plan. I keep losing my place when I look away."

"Good idea. We don't want to be here *all* day." Tomcat cocked his head as if listening for the whir and click of the town hall cluckoo clock that was housed somewhere in the roof space above them. "You are going to the mayor's welcome breakfast for your brother Merlin, aren't you?"

Ella shuffled the notes and avoided Tomcat's bright green eyes.

"Oh, Ella, come on! He's your brother. You have to go!"

"I will go *if* there's time. I rather think preparing my first lessons in magic is more important than watching everyone pat Merlin's back, don't you?"

Tomcat sighed and mumbled something about *the joys of family*. Ella didn't listen. Tomcat had been an orphan back when he was in his human form of Tom April. The naïve lad had idealised views of family—not having to endure one of his own. Ella's eccentric family members were always creating problems she then had to resolve. One day he would have his own family, and then Ella would pipe up: *I told you so*. Until then, she held her tongue.

Tomcat pawed the lesson Ella had prepared. "Gosh, your handwriting is hard to read. Ahem. There are four states of wyld magic. Plants. Elements—"

"Not so fast, not so fast," Ella muttered, waving a hand to slow him. "Where's the R? I saw it but a moment ago..."

"Maybe we should hire someone who can touch-type?" Tomcat suggested. "Queen Sibylla's amnesty on magic only lasts a month."

"What is *touch-type*?" Ella asked as she laboriously sought and then struck the keys one by one and the minutes slouched by.

Tomcat mimed tapping keys with his paws. "It means you don't look at your fingers as you type. You just focus on whatever you're copying out."

"Ha! Nonsense! You fooled me for a moment... Besides, I'm nearly done with the first paragraph! I think I have a natural talent for this skill!" The cluckoo clock in the town hall tower above them chimed. "Listen. It's only a quarter past eight. Plenty of time to get to Merlin's *tedious* breakfast." Ella grinned despite herself. "Come see what I've written already."

"Taking ten minutes to type a single paragraph doesn't make you a natural..." Tomcat's fluffy tail obscured the typewriter as he wound around the contraption to scrutinise her morning's work. His cat whiskers fanned out. "They say you learn something every day! *Ha ha!*" And he clutched his round little tummy in laughter. "You've typed: There are four states of wyld magic pants! *Pants!* Not plants!"

"Oh, bother!" Ella pushed the cat out of the way and peered at the glaring error written in black for all to see. "How do I make it go back and add in the L?"

"Ella! This is a typewriter, not magic!"

Ella placed her wrinkled hands on her narrow hips. "What good is it, then?" She huffed out a breath of disdain. "I don't see what the fuss is about. Foolish modern contraption."

Tomcat waved a paw. "Maybe you just need to put fresh pants on and it will all be magically better!"

"Yes, yes, hilarious," Ella grumbled, but thankfully, before Tom could utter more foolishness, there was a tentative knock on the glass door of the office. "Saved by the knock," Ella said under her breath and then called, "Come in, my dear."

The door opened and the butcher's young son, Chelton Junior, better known as Cheapcuts, entered the room. He was wearing a very fine suit jacket that was several sizes too large for the gangly boy. "Me ma wants to know if this outfit is good enough for magic schooling?"

He winced on saying the word *magic* out loud and even looked over his shoulder as if frightened of being overheard. It was no wonder. For the past twenty years, Queen Sibylla had prohibited the use of magic within Wyld Kingdom on the pain of death.

Ella walked around the boy as he held out his arms for inspection. Not only was the jacket far too large, the suit trousers appeared to have been altered to the correct length, probably by Martha, the boy's mother. "How old are you now, Cheapcuts?"

"Fifteen." And he ducked his head, his usually cheerful expression darkened with an uncharacteristic moment of worry. "I ain't too old to learn, am I? I promise I'll work extra hard." Tomcat leapt off the desk and wound around the very dead potted plant that was part of the *waiting area* inside the office door.

Ella patted the boy's shoulder. "You are well within the age group suited for tutorage, my dear. I was just wondering. Is this extremely fine suit something your parents hoped you'd grow into?"

The boy bobbed his head in time with every honorific as he replied, "Aye, Missus Good Mother, Your Ladyship. Me ma says I might need it for when I get apprenticed to a magician or such like."

"Your mother is a sensible woman," Ella replied, "but for lessons tomorrow, your usual attire will suffice. Save the suit for a grander occasion."

"Yes, ma'am, Your Ladyship's Highness." Cheapcuts crossed both sets of index fingers and touched his earlobes in what had become a secret salute among the local children that Ella had observed possessed some natural innate magic. He skipped back out of the room, yelling, "See yer tomorrow at the unicorn fountain! Strike o' noon." Which was the designated time and place Ella had spread the word to meet for their first lesson.

Ella wiped her palms on her long, black skirt. "Lessons, right, back to the lesson plan." To think she held the hopes of so many good people's children's futures in her hands!

"You'll do fine," Tomcat said, blinking up at her as if reading her mind. "Don't worry."

She allowed herself a moment of self pity. "Oh, Tom, what if I'm a terrible teacher? What if I can't help them identify their talents and their wyld magic fades away with no one to guide them?"

Tomcat scampered up onto the desktop and placed a furry paw on either side of her face. "I believe in you! And let's not forget, Willow said she'd come and help." His tail flicked, as if something was also troubling him. "Do you think I could join in the lessons, too? Please? It would be super cool to wave a wand and go, ta-*dah!*"

"Remind me, how old are you?"

"Twenty three-ish. The orphanage wasn't sure." His little shoulders rounded. "Does age matter? Is that why you asked Cheapcuts?"

Ella chewed on her bottom lip and turned away to survey the snow-dusted view of the pretty stone and tile buildings that made up Charmington's Northgate Square far below the town hall attic in which they stood. "Without training, most human children lose any innate Wyld magic they may possess at puberty. But some, like Cheapcuts who have a witch or other magical type within their family tree, can have their magic blossom again when they are much older, provided they receive the *right* training."

"I don't know my family tree," Tom said, whiskers drooping.

Ella placed a finger under his chin so he would look at her. "Then anything is possible." She nodded. "And you *are* a talking cat. You do possess magic, even if it's temporarily borrowed from the natural wyld magic in my pumpkin patch..."

Tomcat's whiskers fanned hopefully but before he could speak, a male voice piped up, "Hey, hey, Smella! There's my favourite little sister!" She spun around to see her brother Merlin had snuck into the attic office.

"Give your famous big brother a hug!" Merlin said, doing just that and wrapping his arms around her. "Gosh, you've aged badly in the years we've been apart!"

"Why aren't you wearing your respectable blue wizard's robe?" Ella snapped, extracting herself from his embrace, and gawked at the unusual black leather garment he wore. "What a peculiar jerkin. You look like a rogue." Ella huffed, crossing her arms. "Like one of those chaps who robs stagecoaches."

"Exactly!" Merlin said, his grey eyes twinkling. He ran a hand through his tousled black hair and made a show of straightening the sleeves of the jerkin and then tugged up the collar. "You're so old-fashioned! It's not a *jerkin*, it's called a *leather jacket*. Gwen says it makes me look *on trend*. Gotta play to the crowds when you're a celeb—not that you'd know, little sis."

"You're Merlin!" Tomcat breathed in awe, his little pink mouth agape. "You wrote *The Guide to Magical Creatures of Wyld Kingdom*—I love that encyclopaedia! I've read *every* word."

Merlin snapped his fingers. "Always pleased to meet a fan. How about an autograph for the cat?"

"He doesn't want an autograph," Ella grumbled at Merlin, who, in his entitled manner, snatched up her handwritten lesson plan without asking for permission.

"Yes, I do!" Tomcat said, darting off the table and heading to the door with a, "I gotta fetch my friend Cassidy. She'll want to meet you too!"

"Still a shameless old show off, I see," Ella tutted at her brother while she tapped her toe against the floorboards. "Barging in unannounced and bamboozling my soft-hearted friend. Why are you here anyway? Shouldn't you be downstairs lapping up the praise of the guests at the breakfast the mayor is holding in your honour?"

"First rule of show biz, a *late* entrance makes a *great* entrance," Merlin quipped then said, "Sibs told me you'd be hiding out up here—she didn't tell me you had a talking cat though. Now that is an impressive spell! And quite a step up from the boring old pumpkin magic you used to be obsessed with."

"That's because Sibylla doesn't know about the talking cat," Ella confessed tightly. "And I'd prefer she didn't find out about him, thank you very much."

Merlin mimed stitching his lips, but then he slapped Ella on her arm with her bunch of handwritten notes. "Anyway, what's this about? Why aren't you using the *Merlin's Magic For Beginners* textbooks I smuggled you?"

Ella let out a breath. "First, you only sent *one set* of books, and I am expecting *a lot* of students this month during the magical amnesty. And second, after reading your verbose and waffly textbooks, I deemed I could write a better and far more succinct lesson plan."

"Ouch!" Merlin clutched at his heart in mock pain. "FYI, people expect the waffle, little sis. Haven't you heard? It's not the steak you sell, it's the sizzle?" Then he peered at the paper wound into the typewriter. "Since when has *pants* been *one* of the states of magic, let alone four?"

A flush of embarrassment scalded Ella's cheeks. "Typing is not as easy as it looks. Here's a use for your endless theatrics, Mr. Show Off. Bespell this infernal contraption for me so it copies out my notes. You should be able to charm these dull iron keys in no time."

Merlin coughed and backed away from the typewriter. "I would, but I've got places to be. Besides, manual spells need constant supervision, otherwise it will type the same line over and over." He caught sight of his reflection in the window glass and reached into his leather jacket. "Wait a tick, got to fix the hair."

He pulled out a comb from his pocket and a small piece of paper fell out and fluttered the table.

"Tell you what. I'll introduce you to Gwen Pendragon. She's my publisher," Merlin muttered, combing his roguishly unkempt hair into more of a mess. "She'll give you as many copies of the *Merlin's Magic For Beginners* textbooks as you need—it would make a great press article. We can quote you saying how marvellous they are! Great promo op. Gwen will love that."

Ella pulled a sour face. She did not want to increase Merlin's self-inflated ego, but more copies of the textbooks would be useful...

While Merlin preened, attention fixed on his reflection, Ella picked up the dropped note to return to her brother. Her eyes flicked to the line of text, typed on the notepaper.

```
Soon everyone worlD wIdE will know your Secret.
```

Ella snorted. Well, she wouldn't be asking Merlin to do any touch-typing if this badly typed rendition was a testament to his skill. "What secret are you peddling now?"

Merlin snatched the note from her. "Nothing. Ignore that, just some foolishness."

"See? It's not pleasant when people read your things without permission, is it?" Ella responded pertly.

"Quite so, Smella. I'll be good from now on." Merlin crossed his heart and nudged Ella. "C'mon, let's go before Sebastian, the mayor, dies of old age. Apparently ol' Seb is going to declare today as 'Merlin Day' in my honour! What do you think of that, huh?"

CHAPTER 2

MERLIN HECKLES DOCTOR HYDE

TOWN HALL, NORTHGATE SQUARE, CHARMINGTON.

"Merlin Day! Huh. Big Show Off Day might be more accurate," Ella scoffed as they left the tax office. She paused at the top of the main staircase that descended from the attic offices down to the public levels within the Charmington town hall. She tucked a strand of grey hair behind her ear. "You might want to go ahead. I am very slow these days."

"How long until the Fairy Council restores your personal magic so you can restore your youth once more?" Merlin asked, tucking his arm under Ella's and escorting her step-by-step down the staircase.

"Thirty years," she muttered, a firm grasp on the railing.

"Thirty!" Merlin groaned, but then joked, "Feels like we'll use up a couple of years on this staircase!"

"Hilarious." Ella kept her eyes focused on each step. At last, they approached the final stretch. "You know, since you're here, you could use some of your magic on my arthritic knees."

Merlin grimaced. "I'd love to, Smella, but you know healing-magic has never been my game. Remember that time I accidentally put the entire castle to sleep when I tried to fix Sib's snoring?"

"My dear lady, if I might be so bold, I can recommend a remedy," a cool male voice interrupted and Ella looked up to see Doctor Hyde on the first floor landing, staring out the round window that overlooked the unicorn water fountain feature. The tall thin man wore his long black duster. His hawkish features, though usually dower, were more so, his stern gaze fixed on her brother. "A daily dose of turmeric and black pepper, consumed in a hot tea, will provide comfort to mild aches and pains."

"Thank you, Doctor. I will try that."

The doctor bowed in front of Ella. "Not at all, Mistress Charming. My thanks again for your generous donation of your flying carpet. The auctioneer said several more bidders registered for tomorrow night's auction and he's sure the carpet will sell for more than enough money to repair the hospital roof."

"Edison Hyde! As I live and breathe!" Merlin blurted, releasing Ella and slapping the doctor on the shoulder, which earned him a truly glacial glare. "Still touting your useless waffle, I see. You don't fix arthritis with hot water! Save that advice for washing the dishes!"

Ella looped her hand under Merlin's elbow and tugged at his leather sleeve. "Come along, Merlin. Unlike you, I'm sure the doctor has *important* matters to attend to."

Ella had met Doctor Hyde last month and learned they shared a united disdain for Merlin's showboating. The doctor had published a book titled *Rare Poisons and Their Antidotes*, at the same time when Merlin's *The Guide to Creatures of Wyld Kingdom* was released. But while Merlin's encyclopaedia had soared in popularity, Doctor Hyde's poisons book had sunk into oblivion.

"Edison, won't you join the breakfast?" Merlin called back as Ella guided him away and he gestured down the stairs to the hallway, where people were streaming into the town hall foyer. "Gwen is here too—you can ask her for a quick update of those sales stats. I bet your wee pamphlet has broken double digits by now!"

"You really are the worst!" Ella hissed as Merlin escorted her down the last of the polished-marble steps to the ground floor. "Why do you have to antagonise everyone?"

Merlin shrugged, casting a glance back at the tall doctor silhouetted against the ornate window overlooking the town hall square. "Don't let Edison's po-faced demeanour fool you," Merlin said, patting her hand. "He's wildly jealous of my success! Ugh—I should've pretended I'd forgotten his name! Next time! Anyway, why did *you* donate your flying carpet to fundraise for the hospital? Isn't that what taxes are for?"

Ella shook her head as the flow of townsfolk swept them up along the grand oak-panelled corridor in a drift towards the main entrance where the town doors were open wide and a red carpet had been rolled out. "Long story short, Charmington is in financial ruins."

"Ruins? That's not possible." Merlin's roguish grin faltered. He dragged her away from the entrance and out a nearby side door that was open to accommodate the flow of people trailing from the icy streets into the warm interior of the town hall. "Financial ruins! What are you talking about?"

Ella blinked in the morning daylight and breathed in the frosty air. "Keep your voice down," she whispered. "We don't want to create a public panic." And she plastered a tight smile across her wrinkled features and bobbed her head to acknowledge a few passing citizens. "But with Sibylla's banning of magic these past twenty years, well, think about it. Our economy was built on magic—the schools, the spas, the goods. It's all gone, you know."

Merlin rubbed his face with his hands. "Okay, look, I didn't want to have to reveal this just yet, but I'm working on something. Something big. It's going to be worth a fortune."

"Merlin! There you are!" cried a curt female voice and an elegant woman with a stylish blonde haircut stormed out of the town hall building towards them.

Ella had never seen a woman other than a guardswoman dressed anything like this lady before. Mid thirties, maybe older, she had a red-leather jerkin—*jacket*—much like Merlin's. Tight doe-skin trousers and boots with heels that looked sharp enough to pierce skin. Gracious, was she Merlin's bodyguard? But the blonde woman wafted perfume, and she had pearls and gold chains at neck and wrists. She dressed to sparkle, to catch attention and not blend in. Clearly, this lady was no bodyguard.

Merlin's shoulders sank, and he scrubbed his face again and then waved a quick introduction between the pair. "Gwen, this is my younger sister, Ella. Ella, Gwen Pendragon, my publisher at Camelot Academy Press, and, er, my current girlfriend..."

Girlfriend, was she? Ella thinned her lips. Dating his own publisher. That hardly seemed ethical. Then again, her brother had always been a bit of 'a player' as the young ones said...

Both women blinked at each other. Gwen took a step back. Her angry exterior turned to confusion for a moment as she took in Ella's appearance. Ella knew the description 'younger sister' did not fit well with Ella's aged and withered body, dressed as she was in widow's black, long woollen skirts and hobnail boots.

"What do you mean, *current?*" Gwen snapped at Merlin, turning her back on Ella. "*Current* girlfriend?"

"It was just a slip of the tongue," Merlin blurted. "Gwenny, sweetheart, dearest. You know you're my one true love."

"Oh really? According to more than one old lady in there, she was your one true love last time you were here. So who is it? Me or one of them?"

Merlin looked over his shoulder in alarm as several town's folk had gathered close. And he waved a hand at the arched bridge walkway that connected a wing of the town hall across the alley. Someone had decorated the walkway bridge along the rails with several black typewriters and swags of blue fabric in some bizarre mimicry of bunting. "Gwen, have you seen this splendid decoration? A writer's walk! How clever! My congratulations to the decorating committee." He clapped loudly and the gawking citizens joined in with a smattering of applause. But then Merlin ducked his head and hissed at Gwen, "Can we discuss this later? Privately?"

Ella rolled her eyes. "Don't mind me," she muttered, leaving the pair to their argument, and she strolled back inside the town hall and crossed the red carpet into the packed main chamber.

Goodness, what a turnout.

Dozens of tables, covered in white linen, filled the large room and there was a buffet lining one wall. While the stage had chairs and a lectern waiting, no one seemed in a rush for the announcements to start. The air was filled with good-humoured chatter and the scent of fresh bread, sausages, eggs, and honey-bark tea. Ella's stomach growled. Well, if she was going to have to be stuck listening to the mayor drone on about Merlin's virtues, she might as well do it from a comfy seat and have a hot-buttered muffin and a cup of tea to help pass the time.

She looked around at the various faces.

Master Chelton, the local butcher, and his wife Martha, parents of young Cheapcuts, sat nearby, dressed in their Sunday best. Over at the buffet table, tall Claude, the bookshop owner, was being his charming, handsome self as always. Claude was flirting with Willow, who owned a neighbouring bakery, and who was also a talented herbalist and witch. Towards the back of the room, there was a table teeming with scrubbed-faced orphans, all supervised by the indomitable Mistress Fairweather. However, there were several familiar faces missing from the swirl of townsfolk. There was no sign of Marge the midwife, or Bron the baker, or even Goldilocks, Queen Sibylla's hairdresser and healer.

Come to think of it, where had young Tom got to?

"Yoo hoo! Yoo hoo!" trilled an elderly lady, wearing a canary-yellow gingham outfit and waving a white lace hanky from a table positioned in front of the stage. "The council member's table is here, Your Highness. I saved you a seat!"

Ah, Sally, one of the haberdashery owners. Sitting with her business partner and elderly twin sister Millie, who wore a lilac dress.

Ella pressed her lips together as she edged through the crowd toward Sally and Millie. With the distraction of Merlin's sudden appearance, she'd forgotten to bring her walking stick when she left the tax office. Her balance wasn't the greatest at the best of times with her troublesome knees, and all these people milling about, calling friends, or darting here and there, to fetch cups of tea, or line up at the buffet, reminded her of her frailty.

Ella swallowed. *Buck up, old girl. If you can learn to type, you can jolly well cross a crowded room without embarrassing yourself by falling flat on your face!*

But suddenly a young person darted under her arm with a greeting of, "Steady there, I got you, Missus Cat Lady." Sally's new ward Olly, grabbed Ella's elbow with somewhat greasy fingers as the orphan also had a fistful of sausages. Olly was dressed likewise to Sally in canary yellow, although Olly's outfit was a charming little cut away jacket and breeches in plush velvet.

Ella and Olly shuffled towards the waiting elderly sisters. Sally was still waving her lace hanky like a lighthouse beacon in a treacherous sea of chairs, tables and feet.

On reaching the table, Olly pulled out a seat which Ella sunk into gratefully. To think she was daunted by merely navigating around a few harmless people when she had faced off with a were-rat and werewolf out in Wyld Enchantment Woods barely two months ago!

"Your Highness, how delighted you must be! Such a turnout for your brother's triumphant return!" Sally trilled. "Merlin is such a beloved member of the Charming lineage!"

"Hmm, yes, well, everyone loves a free breakfast. On that much, we agree," Ella replied.

"Indeed," Millie responded tightly, crushing a lace hanky into her withered grip.

"Oh, Millie, *tush!* Don't be such a sour sop," Sally scolded. "Merlin broke your heart fifty years ago. Let it go. Must you always dwell on the past?"

CHAPTER 3

THE CRUSH

TOWN HALL, NORTHGATE SQUARE, CHARMINGTON.

Expression stony, Millie lurched to her feet. "My apologies, your ladyship. I forgot...an errand I must attend." The elderly woman bobbed a curtsey and stormed off in a lavender scented wake before Ella could respond.

Sally just rolled her eyes at her twin. "You will forgive her, I'm sure. Millie's always been overly sensitive. I told her, Merlin won't even remember you."

Ella raised her eyebrows. "Speaking of rogues, is Sheriff Axel joining our table?" She looked around the room to change the topic.

Despite Sally's claim that the table, set with silver cutlery and pretty china, was reserved for the council members, only Sally and her ward Olly were the current occupants now Millie had left. Of course, Harold Harper the Postmaster wouldn't be here—considering what Ella had uncovered about him last month! And no doubt the mayor, Sebastian, would be up on the stage once the announcements started. But that still left Axel Luther, the sheriff.

Ah! There was Axel, pushing in line at the head of the buffet, and piling his plate high with bacon and eggs. Hopefully, he would sit elsewhere. Ella trusted the sheriff as much as she trusted a fox with a basket of ducklings.

"Excuse me, Lady Ella?"

Ella turned as someone approached through the throng. Tobias the school master stood there, anxiety plastered across his pale face.

"Master Tobias!" Sally trilled. "Have you told Lady Ella your good news? Tobias has had one of his romance stories accepted for publication!"

"My congratulations," Ella offered. That was good news. The poor man had been trying rather desperately to be published for some time...

"Thank you, thank you, most kind." The schoolmaster smoothed the thinning ginger hair at his temples and adjusted his bowtie. "I don't mean to impose, but I just don't know who else to ask!"

He gestured towards a display of Merlin's *Guide's* piled up in an artful arrangement on the table beside a large silver tea urn.

"Yes, I'm sure you can help yourself to a book." She turned to Sally for support. "Those copies are free, right?"

Tobias chuckled. "Thank you, no. I already have a copy—a first edition!" he added proudly, puffing out his narrow chest. "It's just, I forgot to bring it with me! I want to get it signed!" He looked around at the lectern and then at the round cluckoo clock hung over the doorway. "The speeches are supposed to start at nine. Do I have time to go back and fetch my copy for signing?"

"Yes, yes," Ella muttered, though the time was ten to nine. "These things are always wretchedly slow to get going. If it kicks off before nine-thirty, it will be a miracle."

"Okay! Thank you!" he half-bowed before darting off.

Why was everyone so enamoured by her wretched brother and his annoying book?

"You know, originally it was supposed to be a collaborative effort," Ella grumbled aside to Sally and Olly. "It was going to be *The Guide to Creatures* and Plants *of Wyld Kingdom*. And plants! Only Merlin decided no one wanted to read my, quote, '*boring* treatise' on the various strains of magical pumpkins within our fair kingdom."

"Oh, Your Highness, you don't have your chain of office?" Sally cried suddenly and patted her own throat in demonstration.

Ella touched her neckline, feeling for the clink of the chunky golden chain with its unicorn seal. "Never mind. Must have left it upstairs with my walking stick. No harm, I'm sure."

"I can fetch it," Olly volunteered, standing up.

"Fetch my cane too, if you please!" Ella called as the youth zipped away, weaving between the various people with a youthful dexterity that Ella envied.

"Olly is a helpful child," Ella acknowledged to the elderly lady, who was straightening the silver cutlery. Anyone who saw Ella and Sally side-by-side would think they were of the same age. Yet, in truth, Ella was hundreds of years older. Only when her magical abilities had been bound by the fairy council twenty years ago did her youthful looks vanish as her true years flooded back into a body that magic had sustained for so long. "Are things going smoothly with your adoption process of young Olly?"

Sally chewed her bottom lip. "I have one final hurdle next month. Mistress Fairweather, the orphanage matron, requires several character references for the paperwork." Sally nodded to the ruddy-faced woman seated in the back with a plump babe in the nestle in the crook of one arm, a cup of tea *and* a scone somehow balanced her in free hand, while a swarm of children in matching blue and yellow striped jumpers darted back and forth from the buffet to the table like a worker bees hovering about their hive's matriarch.

Ella pressed her fingertips to the back of Sally's hand. "I am happy to oblige. But what of your sister Millie? Can she vouch for you, or can't the referees be family members?" Ella said, looking up at the townsfolk, most of whom had now found their places.

Sally clutched a white linen table napkin and wrung it between her delicate hands as Axel Luther, his plate laden with steaming scrambled eggs and bacon, dropped his battered black tricorn to the tabletop and slunk down at the table across from them without acknowledging either woman. "No, er, Millie didn't feel it would be appropriate...Biased opinion, you know... Millie only does what is proper and respectable. I credit her that much."

At this, Axel smirked. "Oh really? So it wasn't Millie batting her eyelashes and fawning over the mayor outside just now?" he said slyly, while sprinkling salt over his eggs. Axel's eyes lit up with a mischievous cunning. "They were discussing the new tenancy agreement to *her* haberdashery..."

"She, *what*? That artful hussy! It's *my* business!" Sally cried, rising to her feet, a quivering rage of yellow gingham and lace. "I don't care if I forgot to sign the official document! I only invited Millie to be my partner at the time because Merlin had left her and she was annoyingly mopey!" Sally flung the napkin down on the tabletop like a duellist slapping a glove. "I will not be pushed out!"

Last month, the twins were having some disagreement regarding the ownership of their shared haberdashery business, and Ella hoped it had been resolved. Clearly, that was not the case.

Ella frowned at Axel as the other woman marched off through the throng. "That was uncalled for. It's the sheriff's job to maintain the peace, not stir up trouble."

Axel rolled his eyes at her. "If I'm the pot, you're the kettle." And he sat back and put his heavy boots up on one of the unoccupied chairs. "I bet Harold agrees with me."

How rude! And hardly true at all. When was the last time Ella had *deliberately* caused trouble? She was the paradigm of harmony and responsible behaviour. Harold had well and truly dug his own grave!

"Fair warning, Granny Kettle," Axel continued, "you should hand in that talking cat of yours during this month's amnesty on magic." He mopped bread through the bacon fat on his plate. "Because next month, I won't take my eye off of you..."

Ella stood up from the table and mumbled something about fetching a cup of tea. Gracious Axel was a rude oaf. As if he could intimidate her!

She ventured over to the tea urn where Nigella Pickford, a local actress, and proprietor of the Pickford Players theatre company, was in discussion with a blond youth who appeared to be about twelve years old, dressed in lederhosen and with a German-tinged accent.

Ah! Hansel. That was fortunate! Ella had been wanting to have a word with Hansel. She needed someone with a mathematical brain to join the tax team, and Hansel might fit the bill.

"*Ja*, I counted zem myself," Hansel was saying to Nigella as he poured them both a cup of the fragrant honey-bark tea. "One typeviter per dozen railings. One dozen typeviters in total. The archway display has a pleasing ratio." He sipped the tea, little white fangs protruding on the cup rim. Much like Ella's appearance, Hansel's youth was also an illusion, but compared to the many years Ella possessed, Hansel's true age dwarfed them.

"Is that what Sally wanted the typewriters for? Decorations?" Nigella replied, one hand clutching a walking stick. Ella had last seen Nigella at Doctor Hyde's hospital, her leg entirely encased in plaster. It was good that Nigella was now back on her feet. Doctor Hyde was a kind and competent man, and Nigella's recovery was proof.

"Are you discussing the writers' walk?" Ella asked, thinking back to the oddly decorated archway strung with swags of fabric and typewriters and wondering if Merlin might still be out there being berated by that formidable red-jacket woman. That thought made her smile.

"Yes. Sally asked me if I might loan her my typewriter. But I use the thing every other day. I'm rewriting a classic play for my annual Christmas production—we're holding open auditions next month."

Ella's hope perked up. "Oh! Can you type?" To think two of her problems might be solved by this one meeting. "I don't suppose you want a job? You would be compensated." She turned to Hansel. "And I was rather hoping I could persuade you to join the tax team?"

Nigella mumbled something into her teacup about not being very good with numbers, but Hansel stood up straighter and smoothed the front of his little checked shirt. "*Ja!* I vould be most delighted. Zee stagecoach business is in a slump. Admittedly, Gretel is not zee best vith customer service..."

The cluckoo clock above the door began to toll the hour, as did the town hall clock tower outside, and the room reverberated with the crow of mechanical roosters.

Cock-a-doodle-doo! Cock-a-doodle-doo!

All heads turned towards the sound, and suddenly Merlin's silhouette filled the town hall entrance.

"Ugh, showmanship," Ella muttered tightly, but then her brother stumbled inside the double doors, pointing and waving.

Merlin sank to one knee, and a ripple went around the room. Gasps ushered from hundreds of mouths as everyone realised something was wrong.

Into the silence that blanketed the stunned room, Merlin said, "There's been a terrible accident! Half of the writers' walk display gave way! Several typewriters fell!" He clutched a hand to his mouth. "A lady has been crushed."

Chapter 4

Lessons Learned

Unicorn Fountain, Northgate Square, Charmington.

Midday, the Next Day.

"Millie..." Poor Millie.

Millie, who had her heart broken by Merlin decades ago, met her death yesterday in an awful twist of circumstances. Crushed by a tribute to the rogue who had broken her heart...

Ella stared up at the archway. To think that yesterday she had stood here looking at this display of typewriters. A writer's walkway display which Sally had set up to honour Ella's brother, Merlin. A display which had partially collapsed yesterday morning and ended up killing Sally's own sister Millie—who just happened to be walking underneath at the moment it came tumbling down. It was a terrible tragedy.

Cock-a-doodle-doo! Cock-a-doodle-doo!

The sudden crow of the town hall cluckoo clock heralding midday snapped Ella back to her senses. With one last look of regret cast at the remaining typewriters strung across the walkway railings above her, Ella set off at a brisk pace as she could manage, her walking stick tapping along and the chain of office about her neck also jangling in time. "Late for my own class! That won't set a good example!"

Tomcat appeared and fell into step beside her long, swishing skirts. His whiskers fanned as he trotted across the cobbles and his green cat eyes blinked. "Just think, all those minds waiting to be filled up with knowledge!"

Ella halted in mid-step. Frozen with horror. "My notes!" She leaned on her stick and patted her pocket with her free hand. "Magic preserve! I left them in the tax office!" Her fingers curled around the various items stuffed in her pockets, notebook, pumpkin seeds, and she pulled out the crushed paper, slightly sticky from jostling alongside the fresh seeds. "No! Here they are! Thank goodness!" Ella clutched her hand around the unicorn seal that adorned the chain of office and pressed it to her heart, her mouth dry.

Tomcat's tail swayed. "You know what I do when I'm nervous? I sing a little song."

Ella pulled a face and let the golden chain slide through her fingers. "I'm not nervous! Goodness, I don't know why you'd think that!"

Suddenly, Willow rushed up beside Ella. The young woman's various amulets and bracelets jangled as she spoke. "Sorry! I know I said I'd help! I got distracted roasting coffee beans for Doctor Hyde and lost track of the time."

"Nonsense, Willow, my dear, you are right on time. And there's no need if you have more pressing matters. Today's lessons are just fundamentals, to help uncover what latent wyld magic the children might possess. You are already an accomplished witch. You will be terribly bored, I fear..."

Willow's gaze dropped, and she clasped her hands together. "You're very kind to assume that. But to be honest, I was too embarrassed to say before... But you see, I had no formal training! I learned everything I know from my granny! I was planning on listening-in to all your lessons. I won't get in the way. I'll just stand at the back."

"Ooh!" Tomcat's tail stood on end and cat eyes blinked up at Ella. "Me too! Me too! Don't forget me. I said yesterday that I want to learn magic!"

Ella narrowed her eyes. Were they actually genuine in their intent, or just trying to bolster her confidence? "Very well," Ella relented. "Willow, having you as my teacher's assistant would be much appreciated and anything you don't know, you soon will. And Tom, yes, you may join the children."

"Thank you!" Willow said. The young witch looped her hand into the crook of Ella's elbow and gave her a squeeze. "Oh! Isn't this exciting! I feel like I'm witnessing history! The dawn of a new era!"

"Hardly!" Ella cocked an eyebrow at the pair. "I don't understand what all the fuss is about." But she allowed herself a moment of pleasure at the young woman's enthusiasm as they fell in step, adding, "Don't thank me yet, Willow. We'll be exhausted by the end of the day if there are dozens of children..." They rounded the corner and approached the unicorn fountain in Northgate Square and the glow of smugness faded. Only three children awaited.

"It's Cheapcuts, Sam, and Sandy!" Tomcat darted off ahead, running up to Cheapcuts the Butcher's boy, who stood hunched beside two of the Baker Street orphans whom Ella recognised. The two blonde orphan siblings both wore their familiar knitted jumpers in striped blue and yellow. Sandy had shoulder-length blond hair. He had a snowball on his palm, held aloft as if showing it off to Cheapcuts. The other orphan child, Sam, had cropped hair. Sam's jersey bulged at her shoulder and a large white rat peaked out from the neckline of the child's jumper and then burrowed back down out of sight.

Ella gripped the silver head of her walking stick and slowed her steps as she glanced around the town square. "So few..? I thought there'd be a lot of children."

Willow sighed. "I'm afraid there's a nasty rumour going around that Queen Sibylla's magic amnesty is a trap..."

"I see." Ella pressed her lips together. "And parents are afraid of dire repercussions for their children next month when my sister Sibylla reinstates the ban on magic?" Ella glared at the castle in the distance behind the town hall.

"Something like that." Willow bowed her head, her orange hair falling in her eyes. "I told people you'd never do such a mean thing! Truly I did."

Ella shook her head, the sting of disappointment giving way to her stoic resolve. She swallowed and smoothed her skirts. "Hold your head high, old girl," she muttered under her breath. "Very well, I shall make sure that while I can, these children at least will receive a solid grounding in the fundamentals."

Willow's eyes lifted to meet Ella's, and she nodded, her expression a mixture of hope and grim determination. Willow couldn't suppress her grin. "Welcome to history."

Her mood lifted and her resolve hardened, Ella tucked the gaudy chain of office under her cloak neckline and strode over to join the two orphan children, Sandy and Sam, along with Cheapcuts and Tomcat at the edge of the frozen unicorn fountain.

"Good morning, children," Ella said, while gesturing to the young witch, Willow, in her colourful patchwork coat. "Miss Willow will also assist with...er, these *special* lessons."

The children all nudged each other, their bright youthful faces grinning in barely suppressed delight. They crossed their index fingers and touched their earlobes. A secret salute to magic.

Ella returned the gesture, and her heart swelled. Perhaps Willow was right. Today might be a day for making history. Perhaps even the first day of the return to magic in Wyld Kingdom? Started from a handful of children and a talking cat? After all, several months ago Ella had been witness to a prophecy delivered by the Queen's own magic mirror—which had claimed Sibylla's rule was to end... Although Ella had yet to see proof that such a change was in the air...

Ella shook her head. She was getting ahead of herself. First things first. Ella leaned on her walking stick and cleared her throat and then glanced at her handwritten notes. "Today we cover the fundamentals of magic...There are four states of natural wyld magic. Plants. Elements. Animals. And last, minerals. Upon determining which attributes a candidate possesses, these fundamentals may be further graded from burgeoning to astute. This will provide guidance in designing a curriculum of learning for those who display an aptitude in said disciplines."

The children's enthusiastic grins crumbled, and they stared at her with wide-open mouths in abject horror, before casting confused glances between each other. Ella frowned at her notes. This wasn't quite the reaction she had hoped for...

Willow coughed politely. "What Lady Ella means is she needs to find out *what kind* of magic you're naturally good at and *how strong* your magic is. Then she can figure out how best to teach you." She ducked her head apologetically to Ella. "Sorry. I'm just repeating what you said..."

"Don't apologise, you are correct." And far more to the point, Willow had understood her youthful audience. She wasn't here to address the elders of the fairy council, after all. Ella sighed. So much for Merlin's advice about selling the steak by the sizzle! She stuffed her grandiose notes back in her pocket and clapped her hands. "Yes, first we figure out *what kind* of wyld magic you have. If any. It's not a competition, there's no right or wrong answer. It's just like...er..."

"If you have brown hair or red?" Willow shrugged.

"Oh, or like pork or beef?" Cheapcuts the butcher's son added.

"Or are left-pawed or right?" Tomcat said, nodding along.

Ella agreed, pointing with her cane. "Yes, exactly. And let's start there. Tom has given me an idea. Animal magic. Does anyone think they might have animal magic? Who can communicate with animals?"

All three children immediately raised their hands.

Ella grinned. Well, that was a promising start. "Which animals in particular?"

All the children pointed to Tomcat.

"Can anyone understand animals *besides* Tom?" Ella amended wearily.

Sam's hand shot up. "Ooh! Ooh!" She waved her hand. "Me, me, me, pick me!"

"Yes, Sam?" Ella asked as the young orphan jumped on the spot and their pet rat's nose poked out the neckline of her jersey. The white rat squeaked loudly from her shoulder and then darted up and gave the child's earlobe a nip.

"Ouch!" Sam clutched her ear. Face flushed, she added, "Mr. Rat talks to me *all* the time! Mostly about workers' rights."

Cheapcuts' face changed from confusion to wonder and he pointed at the white rat. "Mr. Rat is complaining about his sleep being interrupted!"

"I can't understand Mr. Rat. Maybe I'm too far away?" Tomcat said, placing his paws up on Sam's knees. "Can you lift Mr. Rat closer to me?" Tom's cat mouth split into a wide, sharp-toothed grin. Mr. Rat squeaked and fled back under Sam's jumper. "Aww, he's afraid because I look like a cat! How can I do the test if Mr. Rat thinks I'll eat him?"

Sandy, who had crossed his arms, pointed at Tomcat. "I only hear Tom complaining, not the rat." The orphan looked at Ella with downcast eyes. "That means I don't have any animal magic? Don't it?"

Ella placed a kindly hand on the young orphan's shoulder. "I don't have animal magic either. Don't feel bad, Sandy. I rather think you might have elemental magic, the power over water or fire. How long can you keep a snowball in your pocket without it melting?"

Sandy extracted the snowball that he had been showing off to Cheapcuts and scratched his head. "Dunno. Made this here one yesterday."

"Ella, what kind of wyld magic do you have?" Tomcat asked as he perched on the lip of the fountain, his white tail flicking across the stone.

"I started off with plant magic. Later, I studied academic magic, and that's how I earned my wand." Ella felt around in her pocket and drew out a handful of fresh pumpkin seeds. The children gathered close as she held the sticky seeds in her palm. "Everyone, take a pumpkin seed. Tom, you just watch this part for now."

"Do I miss out because I don't have thumbs?" Tomcat said glumly.

"No," Ella replied, as Cheapcuts and the two orphans reverently selected a pumpkin seed, "it's because you don't have any pockets."

"Now, cup the seed in your palm," Ella told the children, while demonstrating herself. "When you go to sleep tonight, hold the seed just like this, cupped between your hands. And tomorrow morning when you wake up, if the seed has sprouted, that means you have plant magic."

"Do not pop it in your mouth!" Willow added suddenly. "Only hold it in your hand. Don't worry about dropping it while you sleep!"

Ella nodded. That was sound advice. She hadn't thought of such a caution, but that was exactly what a child might do. "Excellent point, thank you, Willow."

"Ooh!" Sam tugged on Ella's sleeve. "Can I please have more seeds? To share with the other orphans at Baker Street?"

"That is a splendid idea," Ella said, extracting the rest from her pockets and distributing them out. "Share them with everyone, please, not just your friends. Magic should be for everyone who wishes to learn."

"If you can give me a supply of pumpkin seeds later on," Willow added. "Other children can come to me at my bakery if they want to try."

"May I pick again?" Cheapcuts said, tugging Ella's sleeve. "This one feels thin."

"Me too!" Sandy added. "I want a big fat one, full of magic."

Ella smiled as the children all had another look and discussed the merits of the various seeds as they all tried to find the most promising looking seed for this task. A weight in her chest felt to have lifted, and she caught Willow smiling knowingly at her. Perhaps she *had* been nervous about delivering her first class, but things were going smoothly now.

"Cassidy!" Tomcat uttered, his whiskers fanning as footsteps approached and Cassidy Turpin, a young guardswoman, whom Tom had a crush on, strode over to the edge of the fountain in the company of a little girl with braided pigtails and who clung to Cassidy's legs with every step.

"Sorry we're late," Cassidy said. Brushing her black fringe back, she gestured to the young child, who ducked behind her. "This is Bethany. She's Betty's great granddaughter. You know, the old lady who owns Betty's Pies on Hot Cockle Lane? Betty asked that I bring her."

Ella smiled, hoping to make the small, shy girl feel at ease. "Good day, Bethany. We met last month, didn't we? You came to my party in the tax office." Ella gestured to the other children and Tom. "Sam and Sandy were also there. Do you remember these children, and Tomcat?"

The shy child twirled a braid around her mittened fingers and cast a quick glance up towards the top windows of the town hall, but otherwise kept her gaze locked on the ground.

Willow held out the selection of pumpkins seeds to Cassidy and Bethany. "We're just choosing a seed. Would you like to take one, Bethany?"

Bethany shook her head, tucked her gloved hands firmly under her arms and darted back behind Cassidy, who said, "I'll pick one for you, shall I?"

"Cass, can you also pick one for me?" Tomcat leapt off his perch and stood in front of the slender young woman. "I don't have any pockets to keep one in!"

"What do we do with these?" Cassidy asked. Crouching down, she offered the seed she had chosen for Bethany, who did not touch it, but just stared at the oval seed with suspicion.

"We'll show you!" said Sam enthusiastically. The orphan siblings and Cheapcuts surrounded Cassidy and started regaling her with the elaborate instructions. Mostly where *not* to stick the seed.

Bethany didn't appear to be listening. She just cautiously watched Tomcat as he wound around Cassidy's legs.

There was something different about Cassidy today. What was it? Ah yes, now that Ella thought about it, this was the first time Ella had seen Cassidy not wearing her usual black leather jerkin and leggings that the town guards wore as their uniform. Last month, Cassidy had suffered a nasty blow to the head while on duty. Perhaps she was having some time off? That would certainly be understandable.

"Shall I explain to Bethany about the purpose of the test?" Willow said, drawing Ella from her thoughts. "And maybe go over the bit about animal magic?"

"Oh yes, you like animals, don't you, Bethany?" Cassidy said to her young charge. "Didn't your granny say you can make sparrows land on your palm?" Bethany stoutly shook her head. Cassidy looked up at Ella and shrugged.

Oh well. Young Bethany was free to progress at her own pace.

Ella turned her attention back to Willow's question. "Yes, do, my dear," Ella said, tapping her cane against the cobbles for emphasis. "You have such a knack with the youngsters. And next, would you please have them find a clean patch of snow and each make a snowball? I'm afraid my back won't allow me to join in. I can't manage the bending and scooping."

While Willow instructed the children to spread out across the town hall steps, Ella leaned against her walking stick while she squinted at her lesson plan again. "Right, where had we got up to... Fundamentals, animals and plants. Hmm, I still need to properly go over the various kinds of elemental magic..."

A small hand tugged Ella's elbow, and she looked down to see young Olly, Sally's ward, was now standing beside her. Unlike the day before, Olly's bright yellow velvet outfit had been replaced with a sombre black. An outfit of mourning.

The black outfit Olly wore appeared rather baggy, and lacked the careful tailoring of the yellow cutaway jacket and breeches, suggesting this ensemble was altered from an adult's larger garment. No doubt fashioned in a hurry, following the unexpected and tragic circumstances of Millie's death yesterday.

"My condolences on your loss, Olly," Ella said. Though Ella could not see the walkway from this side of the town hall, her eyes unbidden sought the direction of the writers' walk. "I knew Millie from when she was a child," Ella continued, addressing young Olly, "and I'm sure in the months you knew her, she had become a beloved aunt to you. Millie would find great comfort in knowing that Sally has you in these difficult times."

Olly bobbed their head, keeping their silence, which was quite out of character for the youngster. Instead, they just turned an envelope over in their hands while staring wistfully at the other children engaged now in rolling snowballs along the steps of the town hall.

"Do you want to join the others? We're learning about different types of magic. Everyone is welcome." Ella waved a hand and then grimaced as she spied Tom was also rolling a snowball. Magic amnesty or not, if Axel caught sight of a cat behaving in such a human manner, she knew the sheriff would attempt to catch him. "Actually, my dear, can you please remind Tom that he's in full view of the police station and Sheriff Axel has a rather large reward out for his capture?"

Olly touched their crossed fingers to their ears, placed the envelope in Ella's hands, and darted off to stand in front of Tom. Shielding the cat, Olly also crouched to make a snowball alongside. "Dear, oh dear," Ella muttered. "To think a nine-year-old has more street smarts than Tom..." Ella blinked at the envelope Olly had given her. Addressed to Ella, it was from Sally. What was this? Was Sally holding a funeral for her sister? So soon?

Ella propped her walking stick against the fountain and then cracked the envelope open. She read the contents written in Sally's shaky cursive and then stared up at the twins' haberdashery. Sally stood in the second-floor window, watching her intently.

The letter read:

Please come at once.
Yesterday was no accident.
Millie was murdered.

CHAPTER 5

ROGUES

UNICORN FOUNTAIN, NORTHGATE SQUARE, CHARMINGTON.

Ella gawked at the handwritten note in horror. "Magic preserve!" Millie murdered? Surely not? Surely the writers' walk display giving way was nothing more than a terrible accident? Death by typewriter was hardly a conventional method to kill someone!

No... Most likely, Sally simply could not accept the bizarre tragedy that had occurred. Ella shook her head and tucked the note into her skirt pocket. Regardless, clearly Sally was distressed, and if Ella might offer some words of comfort, or keep her company in such a time of need, she would do so.

"Willow, my dear," Ella called out, waving her cane to the young woman, who was laughing as the snowball exercise had now evolved into building a large snowman on the steps of the town hall.

"Is everything okay?" Willow uttered, slightly breathless, as she padded down the steps to Ella.

Ella felt in her cloak pocket and extracted the fine leather notebook and pencil that Doctor Hyde had given her last month. She passed notebook and her handwritten lesson plans to the amulet bedecked young woman as Tomcat also joined them at the base of the water feature. "There is an urgent matter I must attend to. I have a list of simple tasks of aptitude for assessing the children on the back of my lesson notes. Can you please follow them and jot down how the children do?"

Willow flipped the notes over and frowned a little at the list of places to visit across town and the various tasks Ella had thought of to test their range of natural magical abilities. "I'm sure I can figure it out..."

"Thank you so much. I'm not sure how long I will be, but I will catch up to you as soon as I can. I am sorry to leave you in the lurch. And please, keep a close eye on young Olly today. Try to keep their mind off of the tragedy of their adopted aunt?"

"Understood." Willow shook off Ella's concerns. "You can count on me." Smiling, she waved farewell and re-joined Cassidy and the children on the steps.

"Is everything okay?" Tomcat asked, blinking up at her. "I was watching you from over there and you turned white as a sheet. Olly said Sally needs your help. Is it regarding funeral arrangements? Shall I come with you?"

"No, no, you stay with Cassidy and the children." Walking cane clenched firmly, Ella started towards the haberdashery building across the square but when Tomcat trotted along after her, Ella felt a sense of relief and whispered down to him, "I hope it is a misunderstanding, but Sally fears Millie's passing *wasn't* an accident."

"Oh, my goodness!" Tomcat's hackles rose across his spine. "Then I'm definitely coming with you! We're a team, remember! And I may be a cat now, but my heart is still that of a guardsman."

A few minutes later, they reached the back entrance of the twin's business and residence. Ella climbed the steps from the street level up to the porch and tapped her walking stick lightly on the back door.

The door opened a crack and Sally's red-rimmed eye appeared for a second before she flung the door wide. "Oh! Your Highness, thank you—quick, quick, come inside. The rogue might be watching us even now!"

"Rogue?" Ella muttered as she stepped through the doorway, Tom brushing past her skirts. They followed Sally in her rustling black garment along the hallway and into the lavender-scented back rooms of the twins' haberdashery.

Ella had been here only a month ago, but much had changed. Someone had swept the broad cutting table free of its usual detritus of ribbons, hat-forms, and silk flowers. Colourful ribbons and laces lay scattered about the carpet surrounding the table. Sally sunk into a chair and dabbed her running eyes and nose with a lace hanky which was already quite sodden. "Forgive the mess..." The elderly lady, dressed in black crepe, half-stood and gazed towards the sideboard where a polished silver hot water urn stood, quite cold. "Tea? I should make tea..?"

Setting her walking stick aside, Ella untied her cloak strings, and then hung the cloak on a brass hook behind the door. She placed a hand on Sally's shoulder and gently but firmly guided the old woman back to her seat at the table. "Nonsense. Sit yourself down, my dear.

Tell me what troubles you while I make the tea." After checking that the water chamber was full, Ella opened a drawer and found the striker to light the spirits at the base of the grand hot water urn.

Sally burst out a slew of tears and idly reached for Tomcat, who was sitting on the wooden tabletop. "My sister! My dear sister!" the old lady gasped as she petted Tom's white fur. "Some rogue has murdered Millie!"

"Why do you think that?" asked Tom earnestly, leaning in towards Sally, who let out a small shriek and flinched back from the talking cat.

Sally pointed at Ella and then back at Tom. "Does...does your delightful cat understand me? Oh, good gracious, I am all at sixes and sevens! Now I'm imagining talking cats!" Her face crinkled, and she dropped her head upon her folded arms and wept.

Ella frowned at Tom, and then pulled out a seat across from Sally and sat herself down. "Tell me of your concerns. You have my full attention. What makes you think Millie's passing was more than a terrible accident?"

Sally balled a fist around her sodden pathetic little lace hanky and pounded her dainty fist on the table. "I led the decorating committee, and I oversaw all Cole's work on the writers' walk—those typewriters were solidly affixed!" Following this statement, Sally rose to her feet and rifled through a box of lace stacked on the shelves behind the table.

"Cole?" Ella said aside to Tom as his tail swished back and forth across the polished table's surface.

"My odd job man," Sally said over her shoulder. "Aha!" Having found a box of lace handkerchiefs, she extracted a fresh one and returned to the table where she patted Tom some more, which seemed to sooth her agitation. "Cole is above suspicion. He is not the heartless rogue threatening Millie!"

Ella arched an eyebrow. "Are you telling me someone was threatening Millie? Prior to yesterday's, er...tragedy? Why then did Millie not take her concerns to..." Ella turned in her seat and gestured to the front of the building, towards Northgate Square, where the police building lay. "To Sheriff Axel?"

"Report to Axel Luther? Ha!" scoffed Sally, twisting the fresh handkerchief between her wrinkled hands. "Axel may be sheriff now, but as a boy, he used to shoplift from our haberdashery and he's grown-up to be a very un-respectable adult!"

"A fair point..." Ella tilted her head, her thoughts drifting back months ago when she uncovered Axel was having an affair with the baker's wife... "But what of Cassidy Turpin? There is a competent guardswoman, if ever I saw one."

Tomcat's little whiskers drooped, and he said, over his shoulder, "Cass is having time off from work."

Sally stopped petting Tom and looked startled again, but perhaps because of her embolden state from the reprimand of Axel, the elderly lady appeared to shake off her surprise or doubts and added, "Quite so, Master Cat." Then to Ella, Sally said, "Miss Turpin has my full confidence, but the young lady has not been herself following the demise of her colleague." Sally gulped, as if reminded of her own fresh tragedy, and tears leaked from her reddened eyes.

Ella reached out and placed her hand atop the elderly lady's. "I am at your service. How ever I may help, I shall do so."

"Thank you, Your Highness!" squeaked Sally, then drew a deep breath and swallowed. "I can think of no-one else better suited to getting to the bottom of this! Olly and I were both quite impressed with how you revealed that dreadful traitor last month! We spent many nights discussing it. If anyone can solve Millie's murder, it is you!"

"I'll help too! Everyone loved Millie," Tom uttered, which, though said in support, sent Sally into a flood of tears and hiccups. While Sally fought to compose herself, Ella attended to the hot water urn and added fresh tea leaves to a waiting pot.

When she had prepared a fragrant cup each and a saucer of tea for Tom, Ella prompted the haberdashery owner to continue. "You believe someone purposefully tampered with the typewriter display and waited for Millie to walk underneath?"

Sally sipped her tea and set the cup back down. "Yes. There's no other explanation! A letter arrived for her, and it was clear the contents upset Millie, so I confess I secretly read it. I was sure it was from the mayor, informing her he had sided with me, you see? That we are equal partners in the business."

Ella pursed her lips. The elderly sisters had not been on the best of terms recently, but Ella was not sure of the circumstances, other than Millie had taken the step to check if Sally had signed their original deed of tenancy for their haberdashery. Ella had found the old document and seen the answer for herself. Though the deed named them both as owners of the business, it turned out that Sally had not signed the official deed.

"What did the upsetting letter actually say?" Tomcat asked, his hackles rising.

"I forget the exact wording," Sally muttered, absently patting Tomcat's hackles back down. "It was something like, bring me the *Red Riding Hood* manuscript or else I will tell the world your secret."

Ella blinked. On standing, she walked over to her cloak hanging on the back of the door. "I should take some notes..." before recalling that she had loaned the fine notebook that Doctor Hyde had given her, so Willow could make observations on the children's wyld magical abilities.

Ella sat back at the table. Never mind, note taking probably wasn't necessary. Surely, she would remember any important details Sally shared? "And what is this *secret* the note writer refers to? Do you know?"

"Yes..." Sally chewed her bottom lip for a moment. "I suspect Millie knew the true identity of the anonymous romance author of *Cinderella*."

Both Ella and Tom shared a surprised look. The mysterious author of the popular romance had been the talk of many conversations of gossip throughout their township. Ella narrowed her eyes. Just last month she had a conversation with Claude, the handsome bookshop owner on Fifth Street, and he even had the nerve to hint that *he* was the author...

"Millie once had an early draft of *Cinderella,* years ago," Sally continued. "That's what made me think she knew the author's true identity." She sighed. "And last month Millie was bragging to everyone at Your Highnesses office party just last month, how she had a signed first edition of *Cinderella*. You know, the hardbacks with the wrong cover?" Sally idly stirred a spoonful of sugar into her teacup. "I'm sure she was trying to impress Tobias, or maybe even that new Doctor Hyde chap. He wrote a book too, you know."

Ella nodded. "Yes, on poisons. I've seen a copy. Doctor Hyde showed it to me when we met recently." Not to mention her brother Merlin had been taunting the good doctor with his poisons book's low sales compared to Merlin's encyclopaedia only the previous morning.

Sally sighed. "Millie has always had a soft spot for authors. Worships the ground they walk on... Although she was a bit miffed when Master Tobias didn't want to join our *amateur* book club."

"*Cinderella* is such a good romance story!" Tomcat breathed and curled his tail about him. "My favourite part is when Cinderella battles the pirate king to save the baby goat!" He hitched a paw at Ella. "She hasn't read it."

Ella blanched. "Now isn't the time for your tattle-tales, thank you!"

"But *Cinderella* was our Book Club book of the month two months ago! Your Highnesses elegant and articulate observations on the possible shortness of the prince, was most fascinating!" Sally's wrinkled face opened wide with a hurt, confused look that hinted at betrayal.

"And the *Red* er...*Hood* manuscript? Why did the anonymous letter writer want it?" Ella prompted, trying to keep the conversation on track. "What does that have to do with whoever wrote *Cinderella*?"

Sally waved off whatever doubts she now harboured about Ella's reliability as a book club member. "Recently, a manuscript—titled *Red Riding Hood*—had been on her bedside table. I paid it no mind because I assumed it must be another one of Tobias' dreadful works—how he actually got a novel accepted for publication is beyond me! But anyway, now I suspect this *Red* manuscript must actually be the long awaited *Cinderella* sequel!"

Tom gasped, but Ella was at a loss. "And...so?"

"This mystery person threatened Millie. Forced her to give them the manuscript! And then to cover their tracks, they waited until she walked under the writers' walk and killed her! It may have looked like a terrible accident, but the timing is too suspicious."

Tomcat paced about the table. "Sally's right! A *Cinderella* sequel would be worth a fortune!"

"But why would they kill her if she *gave* them the manuscript?"

"I said! To cover their tracks!" Sally flapped her hands. "In case Millie decided to risk exposing her secret and report them."

Ella asked, "Could it be that Millie herself was the author of *Cinderella*?"

"Ha!" Sally dismissed Ella's implication, stating, "As if Millie could devise such a brilliant plot—she copied *all* my hat designs, you know!"

"Do you know where the letter is now?" Ella said. "You didn't recognise the handwriting?"

Tom leaned forward. "Yes! If it wasn't signed, perhaps we can at least compare handwriting?"

Sally snorted. "Alas, the cunning rogue typed the note. Though I thought nothing of it at the time... Now I understand why they did so." Sally pressed her fingertips to her lips. "And I'm afraid I can't show you because I gave the note to Merlin. Last night, he came by to offer condolences—as well he should! He broke Millie's heart years ago, you know! Poor lass, she actually thought he would marry her..." Sally's eyes went misty, but then she drew herself together. "I thought Merlin could..." Sally waved her hand over the table. "You know, divine the typist with his magic. He said it would take some time, and that he'd have to get back to me. Only now I fear I can't leave the house until I know who wrote it."

Ella sat back and shared a look with Tom. "You imply whoever wrote it is an acquaintance and they were afraid you or Millie would recognise them by their handwriting?"

Sally met Ella's eye. "This is why I can trust no one! Surely the rogue is known to me!"

"Or, at least known to Millie," Tomcat interrupted. "Let's not forget the threatening letter was addressed to her. They couldn't anticipate you'd read it, especially as you guys were feuding over the tenancy agreement to the haberdashery."

Sally drew back a little and stared at her hands. "Quite so... Addressed to Millie."

CHAPTER 6

OBSERVATIONS AND CONJECTURE

TWIN'S HABERDASHERY, MERCER LANE, CHARMINGTON.

After promising Sally they would do their best to find out the truth behind Millie's tragic demise, Ella and Tomcat ventured out onto the back porch of the haberdashery.

Ella stood on the porch, staring off into space as she tied her cloak securely about her neck.

"What are you thinking?" Tomcat asked, perched on the top step. "You've got your squinty clue-detection face on."

Ella drew a breath and fanned out a cloud of steam in the frosty air. "There's something bugging me, but for the life of me, I can't think what. I feel I've missed something... Do you mind reciting back what we learned?"

Tomcat puffed out his fluffy chest. "My pleasure. Point one. Millie received a threatening note. Bring the *Red Riding Hood* manuscript or else her secret would be exposed."

"Right..." Ella held up one finger. "Clue one. Threatening note. Exchange *Red* manuscript for their silence..."

Tomcat paced back and forth. "Two and three. Millie is killed. The manuscript is taken."

Ella unfurled two more fingers. "And let's not forget point four. Merlin has the threatening letter now, because Sally gave it to him last night."

"Is that even a point?" Tomcat swished his tail. "Surely, anything after Millie's death can't matter? As soon as you bump into Merlin, you can ask him for the letter. Will he really be able to use a spell to find out who typed it? Could we watch, do you think? I would like to see some magic!"

"While I agree with all that, there's something there that feels off." Ella scrunched her eyes shut and thought back to a conversation she had with Doctor Hyde last month. "Avoid conjecture. Observe..." Ella's thoughts drifted back to the scenes of yesterday's breakfast before Millie was crushed to death. "Merlin was rude to Doctor Hyde...then the publisher lady in red was angry...and Sally saved me a seat..."

"What are you muttering?" Tomcat asked.

Ella cracked open her eyes. "It's something Doctor Hyde told me last month. We mustn't speculate. We must only observe accurate details. Accurate... I was thinking about the people yesterday. Who was where? That kind of thing."

"You mean we can't assume the manuscript was stolen because we didn't see it happen?"

Ella folded her hands over the top of her walking stick. "No...hmm. Maybe?"

"Ah! Maybe it's because Sally *told* us the manuscript was taken? But maybe she's assumed that's what happened because the note said to bring it?"

Ella shook her head. "I'm not sure. Anyway, what else? What is indisputable?"

Tomcat tilted his head left and right. "I guess, strictly speaking, we can only observe that Millie has died after being struck by a falling typewriter."

Ella sighed. "Yes...and it's hardly a practical weapon. When you were human, do you think you could have thrown such a bulky item with any degree of accuracy?"

Tom shrugged. "It seems unlikely, but you're forgetting, it wasn't one lone typewriter, one side of the display gave way. A bunch of typewriters fell. Five or six at least."

"Yes, which makes it seem all the more random. Even if someone released the pin or whatever held the display in place, what are the chances of one actually hitting and killing a person?"

"Maybe that's the answer," Tom said quietly. "Whoever typed the threatening note just wanted the manuscript. Perhaps they only meant to scare her into giving it, not harm her."

"And if our hunch is correct, that the note was typed because Millie knew the typist...then how did they plan to get her to hand the manuscript over to them without being identified?"

"Ah!" Tomcat added, his tail upright like a flagpole. "Let's not forget, our knowledge of what the note actually said is down to what Sally remembered! She could have forgotten something. Maybe it said, *leave* the manuscript under the walkway! Maybe the collapse of the display *was* just an accident! Millie was at the wrong place at the wrong time. The display would certainly have weighed a lot. Typewriters are heavy."

Ella hummed to herself. "Yes...the threatening letter. If only we could read the note for ourselves. We shall have to find Merlin so we can read it..."

Tomcat's whiskers suddenly fanned. "Do you think that's what they really wanted with the manuscript, I mean? Just to *read* it? Goodness, *I want* to read the *Cinderella* sequel. Did the baby goat that Cinderella rescued from the pirate king grow up to start its own flock?"

Ella scrunched her nose. "That book sounds ridiculous. Battling pirates and saving goats? Merlin rescued a baby goat once. He thought it was stuck in a ravine but it leapt away when he got down there..." Ella tutted at the memory. "Right, so assuming the collapse of the writers' walk display wasn't just a terrible accident of fate, our suspect is a raving *Cinderella* fan. That rules me out, but you are still a viable suspect..."

"A *Cinderella* fan, or someone who wants to publish the sequel themselves and reap the money!" Tomcat added, eyes bright with the notion.

"I can't believe that," Ella said with a shake of her head. "Just because *we,* the general public, don't know who the author is, surely the publisher must. The publisher isn't going to randomly accept a manuscript claiming to be the *Cinderella* sequel from just anyone. Hmm, although, if it just came down to making money, maybe the publisher could be tempted? No one except the true author would be the wiser, and they couldn't speak out if they genuinely wanted to remain anonymous..."

Tom shrugged. "I don't really know how publishing works. Do you?"

Ella scowled. "No, but ugh. Merlin does. We could always ask him and his publisher since she's here as well. What did he say her name was? Gwen? Or Jen?"

Tomcat's green eyes widened. "Wait! Are you saying Gwen Pendragon of Camelot Academy Press is here? Here in Charmington? Merlin *and* Gwen are here? Oh my goodness! Can you introduce me?"

Ella rolled her eyes. "Maybe it's better we ask Doctor Hyde about the publishing process if you're going to be so embarrassingly star-struck. Anyway, let's go check out the writers' walk and look for signs of tampering before they dismantle the whole thing."

CHAPTER 7

WHAT THE MIDWIFE SAW

Ella stood on the cobbles, looking up at the remaining half of the writers' walk display above where Tomcat climbed and was peering at the six typewriters still affixed to the back railing of the stone bridge walkway that connected two wings of town hall buildings together. The row of typewriters strung along the front railing had completely fallen from the display the morning before, at nine o'clock. The moment Millie had been walking underneath. "Poor Millie," Ella muttered. "Mercifully, it must have been quick."

"She must have thought the whole archway was collapsing, if she had time to think at all." Tomcat nodded. His long whiskers drooped downward. "I can't see signs of anything suspicious," he concluded, jumping down from the stonework. "As Sally said, everything is solidly affixed. On the remaining display side, at least."

"Untimely accident, or impeccably planned murder?" Ella hummed thoughtfully, blinking up at a ripped piece of fabric flapped forlornly in the cold breeze. Echoing the swirl of chaos when tragedy struck the morning before at nine am and the front portion of the display came tumbling down, crushing Millie below. "As ridiculous as it seems, to use such ungainly objects as murder weapons suggests careful forethought..."

In the distance, two guards marched towards them, their unison cry of "Left, left, left right left" only adding to her sense of unease. Her instinct was needling her. *Cinderella... Cinderella... Who wrote Cinderella? Was that knowledge worth killing over? Kill to get possession of an overblown fairy tale?*

"Ridiculous!" Ella muttered and then raised her hand to the two passing castle guards, an older gentleman and a young lady dressed in an ill-fitting uniform. Ella shouted, "You there. Halt!"

The older guard froze in mid step, pivoted about and then snapped off a crisp salute. "Ma'am, yes, ma'am."

But the youthful guardswoman scowled and slouched against the pike she carried. "Buzz off, old lady, we're practising marching," she said, but then the older guard yanked her elbow and hissed something into her ear, which sounded like, 'Beanzister,' but was most likely, 'Queen's sister!'

Ella turned her back on the pair to give the younger woman a moment to compose herself. She inhaled a deep cleansing breath of the fresh mountain air, surveyed the street before them, and then turned back. Two crisp salutes vibrated in the air.

"Secure this area," Ella intoned sharply, and tapped the tip of her walking stick against the cobbles to emphasise her point. "Nothing is to be touched, nothing is to be dismantled from the writers' walk display until I say so. Understood?"

"Ma'am, yes, ma'am," the older guard replied. His young companion, pale-faced, cast a despairing and confused glance at the older man, but then also nodded.

"Thank you. You may get to work guarding this area." Ella waved off the pair and turned away herself, with Tomcat trotting at her side along the frosty pathway.

After a minute of awkward silence, Tomcat said, "I've never heard your royal *bossy* voice before."

"Don't make me use it again," Ella sniffed. "It's not pleasant for anyone." She headed down Mercer Street towards Main Street. Pulling her woollen cloak close to her thin chest, Ella gripped her silver cane head with her free hand. Goodness, to think it had already been a month since Goldi temporarily removed the pain in her arthritic knees.

Had the pain been this bad before? Each step was like a knife stabbing behind her kneecaps—maybe it was from having to climb the town hall staircase to the tax office in the attic every other day?

Despite Merlin's claim he wasn't very good with healing spells, Ella was willing to risk any unusual side effects if it reduced the pain in her joints.

"Ohh, Lady Ella! The look on your face. And you're limping! Are your old bones bothering you?"

A round little dumpling of a woman approached from an alley. Carrying a picnic basket, she had a short red cape. A bunch of blond curls spilled out from under a white hat, framing a pretty doll-like face with wide cherub blue eyes. Marge the midwife.

"Quite. Just a side effect of my age," Ella admitted. "Nothing to fret over."

Marge pointed back the way she'd come along the cobbled alley. "I bumped into Katie just now and she said with the amnesty, Goldilocks has reopened her magical health spa on the upper east side. Goldi could help relieve the pain in your joints, I bet."

"There's a thought!" Ella concluded aloud. "And that explains why I haven't seen Goldi in the last few days. Of course, Goldi would open her magical healing spa for the month of the amnesty."

Marge gestured to the little basket she carried. "I was just bringing some of my butterscotch macarons for poor Sally in her time of need." The round little lady set the basket down and lowered her voice. "Actually, since I have your ear, there's something that has been troubling me..."

Ella arched an eyebrow. Marge's hobby in life was to spread gossip. Could she finally feel remorse for the error of her ways? "What's on your mind, my dear?"

Marge brushed back her curls. "I saw the murderer!" Marge slapped her hands to her cheeks. "Shocking, isn't it? Are you shocked? I'm so shocked."

Ella gave herself a mental shake and resisted exchanging a glance with Tom. "Perhaps you had best elaborate a bit more...? Who did you see, and what do you think they have done?"

"Yesterday morning," Marge launched into her tale, "I was walking across Northgate Square when I saw Millie standing next to a tall, handsome man. She gave him something, a brown bag, and then he ran away! I saw it with my own two eyes! Right before she was killed!"

Ella gripped the head of her walking stick and shared a sharp look with Tom, who was sitting wide mouthed beside the basket. "Did you see him strike her with a typewriter? Or drop it from above?"

Marge stepped back and gave Ella a scathing look, up and down, as if she might be crazy. "Beg pardon? Hit her with a typewriter? He didn't have a typewriter. Who kills someone with a typewriter? Are you having a senior moment?"

Ella sighed. "A typewriter fell from the writers' walk display and it struck and killed Millie."

"Oh! Is that what happened?" Marge intoned in a voice laced with fresh comprehension and she tapped her forehead. "So that's what happened... That's disappointing. I thought he must have stabbed her, and that's why he ran away."

"What time did you see Millie with this man?" Ella asked.

"Maybe eight o'clock?"

That was an hour before the writers' walk collapsed... Most likely nothing to do with the accident. "The gentleman you saw." Tall and handsome... Who did she know who fit that description? "Was the man you saw, Claude? The bookshop owner? Or Wulf, Prince John's bodyguard?"

"It wasn't Wulf." Marge shrugged. "I don't know Claude. Whoever it was, I'm sure I would recognise him if I saw him again from the right angle. I didn't see his face, but his figure was very dashing!"

Hmm, that certainly was true of Claude.

Marge dusted her hands off and picked up her basket. "I guess I don't need to visit Sally then. No matter, the mayor shall have all my macarons. He'll appreciate them since he's holding an afternoon tea at three o'clock to honour that famous Merlin chap. Will I see you there?"

Ella frowned. "I'm sure the mayor can stroke Merlin's ego without my assistance."

"Ha! Lady Ella, you're such a card!" The midwife turned on her heel, her boots clicking jauntily across the stones like she hadn't a care in the world.

Ella had to give herself another mental shake. Gracious Marge was a peculiar character! She seemed to thrive on salacious news and gossip. Hardly the type of visitor that Sally needed when she was already in a state of agitation. Thank goodness Ella had bumped into the midwife before she could upset Sally further with such speculative claims.

Tomcat clawed at her skirt hem and whispered, "Wait! Ask Marge to come find you if she sees the man again—he's still a potential witness to what actually happened!"

Magic preserve! Tom was right. A witness who might settle Sally's mind if he could testify beyond a doubt that the display collapse was nothing but an accident! And Ella would have realised that if she hadn't been so prejudiced against Marge's gossip-mongering habits.

"Marge, wait!" Ella called out to the brisk little midwife. "If you see this mysterious handsome gentleman again, will you come fetch me? At once?"

Marge stopped in tracks, swung back with her eyes narrowed. "Why? What's in it for me?"

"Er, well..." Ella was completely taken aback.

Marge giggled and flounced her hand. "Never mind. We'll call it a favour. You can owe me one." With a wink, she waved farewell and trotted off, whistling as she went.

Ella clasped the head of her walking stick and drew her snug cloak about her shoulders once more. "I have a feeling that's a favour I shall live to regret."

CHAPTER 8

AVALON BOOKS AND STATIONERY

NORTHGATE SQUARE, CHARMINGTON.

"Hmm, where to next?" Ella murmured, rubbing her chin and glancing back at the town hall clock tower in the distance.

"We should go to the mayor's afternoon tea," Tomcat said. "We need to talk to Merlin and get the threatening note Millie received. Remember? Sally told us she had given it to Merlin."

"Yes, but it's over and hour before it starts and all this talk of Claude has got me thinking..." Standing on the intersection of the side alley and Mercer Street, Ella turned about on the spot. Something to do with tall and handsome Claude...

"*What* talk of Claude? You're the only one who mentioned him." Tomcat blinked up at Ella. "Do you fancy him? He flirted with you a lot last month."

"Of course not! I barely know the man." Ella drew herself up to her full height of five-foot nothing and peered down her nose at the cat.

"Love at first sight!" Tom whispered, jumping out of the way of an approaching carriage. "Happens more than you think!"

"Hilarious," Ella muttered idly, crossing the street. Claude's bookshop was on Fifth Street in the upper east side of Charmington. Mercer Street intersected Main Street just along, and if she walked along Main Street, she would come to the Fifth Street intersection shortly thereafter. Nodding to herself, she set off.

"And why do you want to speak with the handsome French bookstore owner whom you definitely don't fancy?" Tom asked with an amused lilt in his voice as he padded alongside.

"Last month, when Claude showed us the first editions of *Cinderella*, he implied he knew exactly who the mysterious author was. Don't you recall? He even hinted that *he* was the author. And if he is, then we can find out if this *Red whatsit Hood* manuscript is even one of his stories. For all we know, Tobias, or even Doctor Hyde, could have written the *Red* story—they are both writers, after all."

Tomcat's ears flicked up. "Yes, Claude did imply that, didn't he? Ella, that is smart thinking. If the *Red* story isn't the true *Cinderella* sequel, it won't be valuable and then it's far more likely Millie's death was just an accident." White paws trotting nimbly along, he picked up his pace. "Did you see Claude at all yesterday?"

Ella lifted the hem of her long skirt as the camber of the street steepened. "Yes, I saw him at the town hall breakfast. Flirting with Willow."

"How did that make you feel? Jealous?"

Ella rolled her eyes. "How long are you going to carry on with this nonsense?"

The cat shrugged. "Haven't decided. You tease me a lot about Cassidy, so it's only fair I have a turn."

FIFTH STREET, EAST SIDE CHARMINGTON.

Fifth Street was a narrow, winding street that edged the grander neighbourhood of East Avenue. Many grand buildings and residences butted up against Fifth Street's collection of odd little shops, mostly antique shops, but it was also home to Willow's bakery and Claude's Avalon Books and Stationery. Ella concentrated on her path and saved her breath for the exertion of the hill climb.

She leaned on her walking stick with a sigh of relief on reaching the bookshop door, and paused to scrape the snow and ice from the soles of her hobnail boots. "Remember, Tom, act like a cat. The fewer people who learn you can talk, the safer you remain."

"Yes, yes," Tom huffed moodily, "no thumbs and no pockets. Not a man. Just a cat..."

"It's for your own good, you know," Ella retorted, and then she pushed the door open into the snug little shop, setting the bell jangling.

Claude's bookshop was a pleasant and quaint space. Every nook and cranny was piled with books or little artefacts, carefully arranged like props on a stage. Even the shop's ceiling was decorated with large playbill posters. A grand empire era desk adorned with glass paperweights and a vase of fresh flowers served as the shop counter. And towards the back, there was a ring of chairs and sofa next to a fat little potbelly stove. There was no sign of Claude, but a group of young men occupied the seating area. They all crowded around Tobias, the ginger-haired schoolmaster, who had his face cupped in his hands.

Ah. An intellectual debate, perhaps? Ella thought as she leaned in and inhaled the aroma of the winter sweet blooms.

And yet...Tobias cut a very forlorn figure surrounded by his chums. Perhaps the teacher had not had his first edition copy of Merlin's *Guide* signed as he had hoped yesterday? But surely missing out on a book signing wasn't the cause for inciting such an atmosphere of tragedy that hung thick on the air, especially when the schoolmaster had achieved his dream of publication? Surely that good news should keep the fellow walking on clouds for some time to come?

One of the young men leaned over from the fat leather chair, on which he perched, and gave Tobias' shoulder a hearty slap. "Upon my honour, you'll get Beauty back!"

Beauty? Who was Beauty? Did Tobias have a lady friend? Ella peered over the bunch of fresh flowers at the group. Oh dear. That could well explain his melancholy. If he'd had his heart broken by this Beauty lass.

"Hold good cheer, my man, Spalding is right!" Another fellow boomed, his voice equally full of somewhat exaggerated cheer. He stood up and placed one foot upon the sofa on which Tobias sat, but then, seemingly unhappy with the pose, crouched before the sofa, like a messenger at the foot of a king. "Command us, sir! We art at thoust aid."

Thoust?

Frowning, Ella turned away as if to examine the window display of special edition copies of Merlin's book *The Guide to Creatures of Wyld Kingdom*, but kept her eyes on the strange bunch of youths with the exaggerated movements. Oh dear, were these odd fellows actors? Or worse, had she interrupted Tobias' writing group? Collectively, there was something peculiar about them that reminded her of brother Merlin's cronies from back in the day.

With a shake of her head, and a reminder it wasn't in *her* nature to listen in on other people's conversations, Ella lifted the silver bell on the desk and gave it a shake. The shimmering chime of the bell was loud in the small space and Tobias' group of odd balls all looked over their shoulders at her for a second, before dismissing her with the casualness of youth.

Tobias, in the meantime, was shaking his head. "No, no, you don't understand." The schoolmaster balled a fist, genuine despair etched on his middle-aged face. "Doctor Hyde told me this morning. In a strange coincidence last night, someone also stole his typewriter!"

Ella straightened. She shared a look with Tom, who had curled about one leg of the elegant mahogany desk. Tomcat tapped a paw twice on the carpet and nodded his head, indicating he had also heard.

"Someone stole your typewriter, Master Tobias?" Ella enquired, setting the bell back in place on the desktop littered with newspaper cuttings all held in place by the glass paperweights.

The youthful men turned her way once more, as Tobias nodded. "Yes! Day before yesterday!"

"And now Doctor Hyde's typewriter has been stolen as well!" the first young man, Spalding, said, his voice clear and strong. And getting to his feet as though he had just announced the crucial line in a play, he turned to his friends, who all waved fists. "What bold midnight thieves sneak through yonder windows and smash the light in writers' hearts?"

Spalding, Spalding... Ella's brain sparked a distant memory. Wasn't Spalding the name of the mayor's grandson? Yes... he was some wannabe playwright and member of the Pickford Players. Ah yes, the young man *was* an actor. That explained a lot.

Spalding gave Tobias another hearty slap on the shoulder. "Though Beauty was captured, the noble writer will...will...?" He nodded encouragingly to the schoolmaster. "What say, ye, man?"

Tobias slumped back into his seat. "It's no use, Spalding, my words don't flow without Beauty!" He cradled his face in his hands once more and the fellows patted his back and shared strained looks. "She was my muse! I'll never write again!"

Magic Preserve! Had the schoolmaster actually *named* his typewriter? What a peculiar fellow. And even more peculiar, how odd to think that someone was stealing typewriters? Whatever for?

"Did you report the theft to Sheriff Axel?" Ella enquired.

"I did, but he told me to quit bothering him," Tobias grumbled, curling his fists. "He said it wasn't a proper crime—he even implied someone had done the world a favour!"

Ella bit her lip to suppress a smile. It wasn't Tobias' fault that his flowery and romantic writing wasn't to everyone's taste, after all.

"Don't let this small piece of bad luck mar the joy of having your story accepted for publication. Sally was telling me yesterday. Everyone is very proud of you."

"Hear, hear," Tobias' chums echoed and slapped their fellow on the back and shoulders.

Ella turned as footsteps approached and Claude's silverfox hair and handsome face appeared from the shelves and rows of books, carrying a dusty old book which he passed to Spalding. "I knew I had a copy! The Scottish play!" But on seeing Ella standing waiting at the desk, suddenly the senior Frenchman's eyes lit up, and he hurried over.

"Forgive Claude, *mademoiselle!*" Claude said in his smooth French accent. "Did I keep you waiting long?"

If Ella shut her eyes for a moment, it was only because she felt dizzy, and certainly not to enjoy Claude's velvety accent wash over her...

"Ahem," Ella began, lowering her gaze to Claude's strong yet manicured and tanned hands, so she wouldn't become distracted by looking deep into the infinite oceans that were his deep blue eyes. "Last month, Master Claude, you implied you were acquainted with the true author of *Cinderella.* I hate to impose upon that knowledge..." Ella risked a peek up to swim in the depths of his eyes. "And at the risk of sounding melodramatic, I confess, it is a matter of life and death."

Claude's liquid cool blues regarded her with careful and earnest attention for a second more and then he clapped his hands and, turning to the group of actors consoling Tobias, called, "Everyone out!"

CHAPTER 9

CINDERELLA PUTS CLAUDE ON THE SPOT

Claude chased the oddball group play-acting at being men from his shop with confident ease, like an ornately plumaged old rooster might chase a flock of young upstarts from his turf.

After flipping the *Open* sign hung on the shop door around to *Closed,* Claude then guided Ella to the seating area that Tobias' group had vacated. Once he settled her on the sofa, Claude ran a hand through the salt and pepper grey of his thick and curly hair, and paced about, his manly composure momentarily melting.

"Forgive me, I didn't mean to put you on the spot…" Ella began, seeing the shopkeeper's consternation.

"*Non, non,*" Claude dismissed her worry and smoothed his thick silver hair before grabbing up the fire poker and giving the embers glowing within the potbelly stove a prod. "I wondered when you would be back to ask that very question."

"You did?" Ella blinked and sat back, resting her hands upon her knees, she sought to share a look with Tom but he was still perched under the shop counter and waved a paw, as if to say, *Don't look at me.*

Ella looked away, Tom had a point, Claude was one of the few people who didn't know Tom could talk, well then, that was to their advantage if the bookshop keeper was hiding something… Marge *had* said Millie was standing with a tall handsome man an hour before she was killed. There was no denying that description fit Claude to a tee.

"Last month," Claude continued, setting the poker back on its hook, and then he sat on the winged-back chair opposite Ella. "I purposefully gave you an opening to say that you also knew the author, as surely I thought you must too…" He shrugged and arranged the sleeves of the cable cardigan that was elegantly draped across his broad shoulders.

Ella frowned. "You thought I must too because…?" Understanding suddenly dawned. "Oh, because the storybook *Cinderella* claims to be based on a true story, and my sister was also named Cinderella! Now I understand."

Claude nodded. "*Oui*, yes, *mademoiselle*." He rubbed a tanned hand across the hint of stubble on his square chin. "But you did not...and so, I have counted down the days until you would return to question me." His deep blue eyes locked on hers.

Gosh, they are piercing. Ella sat back. Her gaze caught the playbills that adorned the bookshop ceiling, playbills that featured Claude—he too had been an actor, and a great one by some accounts. Ella smoothed her skirts across her knees. Certainly, he had a stage presence as they said...

"Yes, I'm aware there are some similarities to my sister's life. She was a princess, and she did meet the love of her life at a midnight ball." Ella swallowed as an old barb stung, as she thought of that moment. The moment Richard—*her Richard*—when his eyes had lighted on Cinderella as she descended the staircase. Ella drew a breath and shook her head at the memory. Richard had never been hers, he only saw her as a friend, nothing more... "But, er, my sister certainly never fought pirates! Gracious, the author must have taken liberties. I confess I haven't read it...entirely."

Under the desk, Tomcat uttered a *ha!* Which he turned into a cough.

Gripping the arm of the sofa with one hand and her walking stick in the other, Ella levered herself to her feet before Claude could offer assistance and make her feel any older than she already did. "So, if you'll just tell me the author's name and where I might find them, I will be on my way."

"*Non*, Claude cannot."

Ella started. "Excuse me?" Before she could spill a fatally arrogant *don't you know who I am?* formed from the wallowing in memories of who she had once been, she shunted aside her false pride and regarded Claude with surprise.

Claude ran his hand once more through his lustrous locks. A look of loyal determination and yet true gentlemanly regret across his handsome features. He bowed. "Forgive me. But my friend..." He darted to the empire desk and drew out a first edition copy of *Cinderella*, flipped it open to a handwritten inscription.

The inscription read: *To my dear truehearted and noble friend.*

"My friend is a man with a reputation he wishes to protect." Claude drew the novel back before Ella could study the handwriting. "He is highly esteemed among the literary academic set, and for anyone to learn of his..." Claude waved a hand at the hardback book. "*Dalliance* in popular fiction, well, it could ruin him."

Ella scowled. "Ruin him?" That hardly seemed likely, but she admired the sentiment that Claude was so faithful to protect his friend. Before she could offer a compromise or promise she would take the knowledge to her grave, Claude raised a finger.

"Ah! Claude has it. I shall write to my friend and let him know of your request. Then if he agrees, he can come to you himself!" Claude rifled around in his desk drawer once more and grabbed out an elegant writing set in black and silver. "Actually, how about, mademoiselle, you write a note and I shall insert it along with mine? Surely, if you entreat him personally, his heart will be moved. He will not deny such a request, if it is indeed a matter of life and death."

He pulled out the spindly leg chair from the desk and Ella assumed the seat while Claude found a fresh piece of parchment for her to write on and cleared a space among the paperweights.

Dipping the pen in the violet ink, Ella tapped the nib against the cut glass ink bottle before writing, *Dear Sir, I require a meeting at once, yours truly, Ella Charming.*

While he peered over her shoulder to scrutinise her note, Ella breathed in the cologne Claude wore. Goodness, he smelled like sandalwood, with just a hint of something else, something delicious. What was it, jasmine? Lemongrass? White carnation?

Claude's breath hissed between his teeth and Ella snapped back to her senses to see him wincing. "Ah, how do you say? My friend is a romantic at heart. Perhaps you could make your plea a little more...poetic?" Claude placed a hand on her shoulder and smiled. "Mention the life and death part. A gentleman's heart is always warm to a beautiful woman that requires help, no?"

"Right, understood. Fancy it up." Ella took another sheet of paper. She drummed her fingertips for a moment and then wrote, *My Dear sir, I humbly request a private meeting. It is a matter of urgency—*

"Add life or death!" Claude interjected.

—truly life or death. Sincerest regards, Ella Charming.

Ella looked up to see Claude rubbing his face in frustration.

"One more time, no? More, more...how do you say...?"

Tomcat sneezed at her feet, a noise that sounded suspiciously like, "Princessy."

Claude glanced down at the cat under the desk, as if confused, but then seemingly dismissed the sneeze as a timely coincidence. "*Oui*, yes! Mademoiselle, you must play the cards that fortune has graced you with. Compliment him with your beauty and status. You should not be shy!"

Ella thinned her lips and grabbed another sheet of clean paper on which she wrote, in her most elaborate cursive handwriting,

> *My dearest sir, I beseech you on a matter of honour, that I may become acquainted with your noble person, in order to avert a disaster in a matter nothing short of life or death.*
> *Warmest regards, Ella Discretion Fortitude Gertrude Charming, right royal princess of Charmington Castle, in the envoy of Wyld Kingdom.*

"Better?"

Claude grabbed up the paper and kissed the air. "Perfection! He will have no option but to grant your heartfelt request. I will add my note and deliver your letter at once!" Ella vacated the seat, and Claude took her place, setting to his task immediately. "Fear not, mademoiselle, I am sure you will have your answer by tomorrow morning if not before!"

CHAPTER 10

THE CLUE IN THE NAME

FIFTH STREET, EAST SIDE CHARMINGTON.

Once they were beyond the shop door and out into the chilly daylight again, Ella huffed a breath of disdain on the mountain air. "Typical! Writers! Needy bunch of ne'er-do-wells. All you have to do is throw them a bit of flattery, and they're all over it like crows to a corpse!"

"C'mon, Ella," Tomcat said, prancing along the cobblestones. "Claude said the Cinderella author has got an academic reputation to protect. It makes sense now that I think about it. I always wondered why they would write a wonderful story but publish it anonymously."

"Academic reputation!" Ella snorted. "I highly doubt that! I can't see someone respectable like...like Doctor Hyde, for example, writing such swill as *Cinderella*. I bet it's just one of those idiots who writes letters to the editor of the *Nottingham Times*—or maybe he *is* the editor of the *Nottingham Times!* There's a thought! That newspaper is mostly fiction, anyway!"

They wound their way, heading back downhill from the crooked little street, Ella's boots scraping on the cobbles as she limped. Tomcat's tail flicked left and right in the air, matching time to the beat of Ella's walking stick tapping along. "That's odd about the typewriters being stolen, wasn't it?" Tom voiced.

Ella stretched her back. "Agreed. I never heard of such a theft before, but then again, I've never paid them any mind. Are typewriters quite valuable?"

Tomcat stroked his chin. "They're costly to purchase, that's true. But being so cumbersome, I can't imagine they're frequently stolen. No wonder Tobias was so upset. If they're being stolen to order, his lightweight model was ideal."

Ella squinted in the bright winter sunlight as she continued her slow descent of the hill. "Ideal? What do you mean?"

"Don't you remember? We saw Tobias outside Claude's shop last month. I noticed at the time because he was carrying a ladies' portable model and I thought he looked odd. And then Willow told us she was renting her typewriter to him."

"Oh dear, so it's not Tobias' typewriter at all—it's Willow's. No wonder he was upset. If he was renting it, then the cost of a new one must be prohibitive for him..." Ella halted and turned to face Tom. "Oh! Do you think Master Tobias can touch-type? We can offer him the use of one of the many typewriters in the tax office, in exchange for a little work." Ella felt around in her skirt pocket for her handwritten magic lesson plan before remembering that she had given the pages to Willow. "Then he can carry on with his romance stories or plays or whatever, and I'll get my lessons nicely typed out."

"Ella!" grumbled Tomcat. He jumped up a pile of crates outside the last antique shop on the corner of the narrow lane where Fifth intersected with the broad width of Main Street so he could speak to her face to face. "I think Mr. Rat might have a few things to say to you about the exploitation of workers!"

"What are you talking about, exploitation?" Ella uttered, baffled. "This would be a beneficial *mutual* exchange of services! Tobias needs a typewriter and I need a typist!" Hands on hips, she huffed out a breath. "How about I *give* Willow one of the tax office machines to settle Tobias' debt to her? Will that solve whatever ethical problem you have with my suggestion?"

"First, they aren't your typewriters to give away as you please!"

"Yes, they are! They belong to the tax office, which belongs to the crown, *my* family." She stomped a boot on the cobbles beneath her boots and then kicked snow at the wall of the little stone shop. "This whole town is Charming property. This road is mine, this adorable little antique shop." She swept her hand across the view of the town hall buildings in the distance. "Everything you see! The town hall! The post office! Mine! Mine! Mine!"

Tomcat's tail twitched sharply. "If Queen Sibylla's understanding of economic principles are as hazy as yours, *Your Highness*, I can see why Charmington is in financial ruin!"

"Hazy? Economic principles! Magic preserve, are you listening to yourself? Whatever is going on with you? You're being very disagreeable this morning." Ella swallowed down a retort and drew a deep breath. "Let's just stop this nonsense before we both say something we regret. Why don't you tell me what's *really* bothering you today?"

"Why do you think something is bothering me?" Tom replied, his ears flat against his head.

Ella crossed her arms. "Because I've never heard you complain about your lack of thumbs so frequently, and you *were* eager to learn magic yesterday because you said, and I quote. 'It would be super cool to wave a wand and go, ta-*dah!*'. Plus, more to the point, I've never seen you miss out on the chance to spend time with Cassidy..." Ella tapped her foot and waited. "Did you two have a quarrel or something?"

Tomcat's shoulders rounded, and his whiskers drooped. "No... It's just she's thinking about moving to Nottingham."

Ella cringed. "Ugh. Whatever for? Nottingham is large and noisy. There's so much crime!"

Tomcat's head bobbed. "Exactly! That's the thing. Sheriff Axel is blocking Cassidy's promotion. She can't grow here. Nottingham has opportunities. Look at Wulf. Prince John has given him a fresh start..."

Ella held her tongue. As far as she knew, Wulf was some kind of assassin or something just as dubious in the employ of the neighbouring regent Prince John. She would hardly call that a fresh start.

She let out a long sigh. "Come along. You can tell me all about it as we walk. Hopefully, Willow and the children are still near the post office. There's little we can do to uncover the circumstances around Millie's threatening note until we speak to Merlin later at the mayor's afternoon tea. Or hear from Claude's author friend in Avalon."

Tomcat nodded and leapt from the crate of boxes onto Main Street, but then he darted back before Ella had taken another step. "Avalon! Claude is writing a letter to Avalon?"

Ella frowned. "I assume so. That's where *Cinderella* was published, wasn't it? Not to mention Claude is from Avalon—Avalon Books and Stationery. The clue is in the name of his shop."

Tomcat's wide green eyes blinked at Ella. "Yes, but Claude said he would deliver your request today and you would get your reply from the author *by tomorrow* if not before! A letter posted to Avalon takes a week there and another week back here to Charmington! Even sent to Nottingham would take a few days! Do you know what this means?"

Ella gasped. "The anonymous author of *Cinderella* is a resident of Charmington!"

CHAPTER 11

THE QUEEN'S CONUNDRUM

INTERSECTION OF FIFTH STREET AND MAIN, EAST-CENTRAL CHARMINGTON.

"Magic preserve. Was Claude lying to me?" Ella pressed the back of her gloved fist to her lips as she turned the events over in her mind. "Was it all an act?"

"What do you mean, *lying*?" Tomcat leaned closer, but occasionally threw a cautionary glance over his shoulder as if worried about being overheard. The intersection of the two streets was not busy, but there were many people strolling the footpaths and wagons and carriages rolling just beyond where they stood on Main Street.

Ella took a few steps further back up Fifth Street and sheltered from sight behind the boxes stacked outside the adorable little antique shop. "I mean, what if Claude was only *pretending* that there is another person involved—what if *he* is the author of *Cinderella*? Claude was an actor of some repute back in Avalon!"

Tomcat cocked his fluffy little head. "I never thought of that!" He leapt back up on the wooden crates so he could look Ella in the eye. "But what about the academic reputation to protect?"

Ella wavered off the question. "Possibly more lies, a cover story of sorts? His description matches what Marge saw after all—a handsome man met with Millie an hour before she was crushed!"

Tom's pointy little ears flicked up and down, alternating left and right, as they did when he was thinking deeply. "I should go back— Claude doesn't know I can talk. I will follow him to the post office or wherever he's headed and try to read the address of the letter he's sending—and if he just circles the buildings, or acts oddly, then we'll have our answer!"

"Agreed! But if he *doesn't* deliver the letter—promise me you won't confront him. We'll take our concerns to Cassidy, or even, dare I say it, Sheriff Axel."

Tom's long white whiskers fanned. "Okay! Good plan. If Cassidy helps us apprehend the person who threatened, if not killed, Millie, then surely Axel can't deny her promotion! Where will you be? Teaching the children?"

Ella nodded. "Yes, so I'll be out and about the town. Or if not—I'll be wherever Merlin is. Let's not forget that Sally said she gave Merlin the threatening note that Millie received. I should still read that letter in case this Claude development is a dead end."

Tomcat sat up straight on the crate and pawed a crisp salute before scampering off back up the winding, narrow little street.

Ella watched him go and then drew her cloak tight across her shoulders and turned back towards Main Street.

To think that her simple concern this morning was worrying if she'd be an adequate teacher. And now she had been swept up into some peculiar happening involving threatening letters and secret identities! It was bizarre enough to be one of the ridiculous scandals that the *Nottingham Times* was always reporting. Thank goodness this sort of thing didn't happen every day.

Lost in her thoughts, Ella didn't pay any attention to the dainty clip-clop of two white horses drawing a very fine carriage down Main Street or she might have also registered the shimmering silver bells that accompanied the Queen's carriage and made a run for it before her sister Queen Sibylla caught sight of her.

"Morning, ma'am," called Dirk Turpin, the royal coachman as Sibylla's coach rolled to a smooth stop a few feet away.

Ella looked up into Dirk's smiling face as he lowered the reins and doffed the tricorn that was part of his royal livery. Besides him, a little white poodle, also wearing a jaunty purple tricorn, sat up and yipped. "Gracious, is that Willow's poodle, Mr. Puddles?"

"Aye, indeed," Dirk answered, petting the little dog as it wagged its tail. "He looks a treat in his wee hat, don't he? Miss Willow thought Mr. Puddles might enjoy spending his afternoons with me, rather than being cooped up in the back of her bakery during the day. He's taken to it like a duck to water."

"I am pleased to see that..." Ella began, but before she could ask another question and enquire after Dirk Turpin's health in recovering from the magical poisoning he suffered last month, the carriage sash window slid down and Queen Sibylla's chestnut-brown locks peaked out. With a most unladylike fashion, she jabbed a finger at Ella and commanded, "Get in! No arguments."

Dirk raised his eyebrows in a sympathetic *what-can-you-do?* motion, before he leapt down from the box. He gallantly offered his hand and then assisted Ella to alight the carriage steps.

As soon as she had settled inside the plush jasmine scented interior Ella braced for whatever scolding her sister had in store. Sibylla's deceptively youthful face frowned and her characteristic snarl pulled her full red lips back over perfect white teeth. "What's this I hear that you're teaching magic?"

"Oh, well," Ella began, a flush heating her cheeks as she brushed her skirts straight across her knees to avoid Sibylla's eye.

"That's a terrible idea! You're a lousy teacher! Don't you recall what happened when we were five?"

"You mean that time you were worried the fish in the Summer garden pond would be cold at night and I taught you a spell to warm the water *gently*. But instead, you *boiled* the pond, killed every goldfish and scalded every duck and somehow *I* got the blame?"

"Yes, exactly! *You* taught me the *wrong* thing to do." Sibylla knocked on the carriage ceiling and then called out, "Drive on."

"I told you the *right* thing to do. Your raw astute magic was simply more powerful than you could handle," Ella replied wanly as the carriage lurched into the motion with a bump and sway. "Putting your out-of-control magic aside for one moment, you'll be pleased to know that I have enlisted a brilliant mathematical brain to help with the financial crisis."

"I will keep that in mind, but I have just found a way out." Sibylla snorted and, rooting around in a little velvet bag at her side, she drew out a golden round powder compact, which she flicked open and passed to Ella. "Fix your face. The cold air makes your complexion positively ruddy—you look like a washerwoman."

Ella glanced at her reflection in the circle of mirror, her familiar features reflected at her in bizarre mockery via her identical twin sister, and the elderly face in the mirror. She snapped the compact closed and tossed it upon the cushions. "If you've found me a rich husband, I think we'll need something stronger than powder to disguise these wrinkles... Did you keep duck fat from the ducks you boiled?"

Sibylla's eyebrows rose. "I may have boiled the pond, but every creature died because you were an incompetent teacher." Her eyes darkened. "Just be grateful the turtle was not in residence..."

Ella frowned. That was an odd thing to say. Why bring up the turtle? The turtle hadn't been a resident of the pond when they were children. Ella assumed Sibylla had only added the creature to the pond in the summer garden after Ella had moved out of the castle twenty years ago. "Remind me again how solving the financial crisis *you* created is worth gloating over?" Ella asked. "That's really why you stopped to pick me up, right? Not to belittle my teaching efforts, but to gloat about your own success? Well, how did you make up for the lost money? Sell the recipe to goldfish-duck soup?"

Sibylla's eyes shone with smugness and she sat back against the lush white furs and plump cushions. "Prince John has made an offer—"

"You can't be serious—marry him? No, you can't. He's so creepy!" Ella's mouth hung open, aghast, and she sat forward. "Magic preserve! You didn't promise him *my* hand in marriage, did you? You spiteful troll!"

Sibylla covered her mouth with a decorative paper fan as she laughed. "Oh! The look on your face!" She snapped the fan closed and tapped Ella's knee with it. "Don't be stupid. Not a marriage proposal—did I say marriage? Why would you jump to such a conclusion—besides, John thinks you're my great aunt or something. As if I would let anyone know I had such an old hag for a sister!" Composing herself once more, Sibylla continued. "No, it's simple. Prince John just wants some of our land—"

"You *cannot* sell a square inch of Wyld Kingdom to that man—to anyone! Are you mad?" Ella crossed her arms tightly. "Wyld magic has a direct connection to our land."

"I know that!" Sibylla huffed out a sigh. "Not sell—*rent*! As if I would sell? Sell to our greedy, magic-hungry neighbours? You are quite ridiculous. No, Prince John just wants to rent several hectares of forest that abut our borders. It will inconvenience no one and solve all of our financial difficulty."

Ella frowned. That sounded too easy. "How can additional rent money solve our entire country's current financial crisis? Twenty years' worth of mismanagement under *your* slovenly leadership can't resolve itself by renting out a few extra hectares of woodland."

Sibylla's sly grin returned. "It can if he pays for the next one hundred years' rent upfront."

"What?" Ella roared, her mind in a spin. "Pay one hundred years' rent upfront? He'll never agree—that's madness!"

"He has agreed—it was his idea," Sibylla returned coolly, glancing out the window.

Ella lurched forward and grabbed her sister's hands in hers, forcing Sibylla to look her in the eye. "*What* does he want the land *for*?"

CHAPTER 12

PRINCE JOHN'S PLAN

QUEEN'S CARRIAGE, EAST AVENUE, UPPER East Side Charmington.

"What does Prince John want to use the woodland for?" Ella repeated her question, squeezing her sister's hands tightly.

Sibylla extracted her hands free with a flick of her wrists. "Don't be such an alarmist. It's nothing sinister. You must have heard the many problems John has been having with his ageing prison. The breakouts and so forth."

"A prison? Build a prison in Wyld Enchantment Woods?" Ella was shocked. "You can't be serious? We can't afford to build that—let alone *think* of building such a monstrosity!"

"That's the beauty of the scheme! *He* will build the facility and manage it. Every brick he'll transport from Sherwood. Charmington residents won't even know it's there. And when the contract expires, the whole thing gets dismantled and removed, piece by piece. There's no downside to us."

"No downside? Please tell me you haven't signed the contract?"

"Though I have every intention of signing..." Sibylla lazily curled a finger about the gauze curtain covering the window. "I am not so foolish as to give John an inkling of our current financial state... I will draw out the agreement talks, so no one suspects I need the money."

"But if I find a better way, will you take it?"

Sibylla's smooth forehead wrinkled with a frown. "You? Find a better way? Such as?"

Ella sat back as the carriage swayed along the roads and shimmering bells herald their progression to the townsfolk. "Well...I don't have a plan as such, but adding Hansel to the tax team must help."

"If you find a better way of refilling the coffers, of course I shall listen. I'm not an idiot." The queen waved a languid hand out the window to some townsfolk bowing along the route the carriage took before catching Ella's eye again. "John is planning his coronation for January, an event which I'm sure will keep him distracted for several months yet."

Ella pulled a face. "I know. I got sent an invite. You?"

The queen rolled her eyes. "Ugh. Yes. Let's not draw straws on who of us must attend as representative yet, but bear in mind, once he is officially crowned King of Sherwood, John will put pressure for the agreement on the prison to be signed. Therefore, John's coronation is our final deadline for having our finances restored."

Ella nodded grimly and counted on her fingers. "September now, so by Christmas we'd better have come up with another viable way."

"Not we, *you*. I have already found the way to ensure my coffers overflow once more. John's prison may not be ideal, but it will pay the bills. I have far too many things on my plate already not to accept such a straightforward solution. You did say you would help me, but what have you actually done? You haven't increased the township rents like I suggested. All you've done is add *one* member to the tax team—which is another civil servant's wage to pay! And what else? Provide the peasants some false hope by teaching magic to their dull children? It's hardly constructive, is it?"

"Oh! That's not fair!" Ella snapped, crushing her skirt fabric between her balled fists at her sister's typically unbalanced assessment of the situation. "If you *permanently* lifted the ban on magic, our kingdom's fortune would be easily restored and you know it!"

"All that would be restored is the constant barrage of fortune hunters and scoundrels trying to get their hooks into everything..." Sibylla cast a glance out the window as the carriage pulled up outside a grand residence. "Here we are, out you pop. You can stand in my stead for the boring mayor's afternoon tea for Merlin today while I attend to more pressing matters of state. And tell Merlin the castle isn't a hotel for his rabble. If he wants his entourage housed, they have to stay within the confines of the East Tower and not wander around like they were last night."

"But the East Tower is mine!" Ella cried, incensed.

"Yes, and it is rather expensive to maintain that wing when you haven't been home for the past twenty years. So, either allow guests usage or give me permission to shut it up—every penny counts, as they say." Sibylla smiled warmly just as Dirk knocked on the carriage door and opened it, his hand held out. The queen cocked her head at Ella. "Out you go, my dear." She blew Ella air-kisses. "Have a lovely time! Don't overeat or you'll get indigestion."

Ella gritted her teeth and bit back a retort as she clasped Dirk's hand and stepped from the confines of the carriage to the crisp daylight reflected off the white-dressed stone of the Mayor's grand East Avenue residence. There was only one reason she was putting up with this nonsense and it was to look over the threatening letter which Millie had received, and then passed on to Merlin by Sally in her attempt to track down whoever wrote it.

CHAPTER 13

THE MAYOR'S LUNCHEON TURNS DEADLY

MAYOR'S RESIDENCE, EAST AVENUE, UPPER EAST SIDE CHARMINGTON.

Once ensconced inside the lavish residence, Ella realised that privately chatting with her brother wouldn't be easily achieved. Merlin was clearly the man of the hour and he and Gwen Pendragon, the woman with the striking red leather jacket and the astonishingly sharpened heeled shoes, were swamped by curious people as everyone milled about a spacious light-filled modern sitting room with an ornate fireplace and heaving buffet table of finger foods. Ella was more than a little surprised to see Sally over by the leafy potted ferns in the corner near the door to the kitchen. Dressed in black, Sally was having a private conversation with Sebastian, the elderly major who was being propped up by his son, a balding fellow with the family beakish nose.

"Your Highness, it is a great pleasure to see you out and about once again," said a welcoming voice. And an elegant woman that was acting as hostess, and most likely the mayor's daughter-in-law, placed a fragrant and dainty china cup of elderberry tea into Ella's hand.

"Thank you, my dear," Ella said, unable to recall the hostesses' name, and stepping back from the buffet table, she inadvertently stood in between the mayor's grandson Spalding, and the schoolmaster Tobias.

Did that mean Tobias had suitably recovered from the theft of his typewriter? Ella wondered. Or perhaps Spalding was merely trying to keep his friend distracted and his spirits up? Ella stood there awkwardly as the pair discussed the Christmas play that Nigella Pickford, the director of the Pickford Players, was planning on putting on that Christmas.

"And what play has Nigella decided upon?" Ella said, seeing a chance to insert herself into the conversation. Ella cast an eye at Sally and the mayor by the potted ferns. Though she couldn't catch any words, from the way Sally was leaning forward, and the mayor was waving a hand and leaning further and further back, it appeared as if they were arguing.

Spalding tapped the side of his nose, a nose that Ella realised wasn't the beakish model that balding father and tottering grandfather possessed. Spalding had a straight, attractive nose like the woman playing hostess, the one who had given Ella her cup of tea, presumably his mother. "My dear ladyship," Spalding said with a chuckle and he nudged Tobias, "Nigella keeps that a close secret. As a keen patron of the arts, you may well enquire, but it is not my place to spill such secrets. Even with your elevated status, your ladyship, you too must wait with bated breath for the announcement next month."

Ella smiled thinly. She was just making polite conversation, after all. Whatever play Nigella chose *next month,* it was hardly going to be *life and death*, was it? It wasn't as if someone was going to write a book about it... She took a sip of her tea and turned slightly to Tobias, who was actually standing on tiptoe, his stare fixed upon the celebrity couple of Merlin and Gwen, lounging at the fireplace and chatting merrily with the many gushing citizens. "And did you get your first edition copy of Merlin's *Guide* signed yesterday?" Ella enquired, privately wondering whether she should quiz Tobias about his touch-typing skills.

Despite Tom's disapproval, she hadn't written off her idea to see if the schoolmaster would want to exchange use of the tax departments typewriters for a little help with copying out her lesson plans... "Would you like me to introduce you to my brother?" She waved a hand at Merlin, who was laughing loudly and hitting a rather tight-faced Doctor Hyde on the back.

Tobias swallowed. "Your...your brother?" His cheeks flushed pink. "Of course, of course, would you? That would be very good of you!" He darted a gaze around the room. "I just need a moment!" And he thrust the teacup he held back upon the table and dashed off.

Spalding chuckled and smoothed his shirtfront. "Forgive my friend. He's a little out of sorts today."

Ella nodded. "Yes, I quite understand. A writer losing their typewriter must be quite traumatic..." She glanced at Sally again, as across the room the mayor extracted himself from her agitated presence as a waiter passed with a silver tray laden with cakes and dainty sandwiches. "I don't suppose you know whether Master Tobias can touch-type?"

"Touch-type?" The young man pushed out his lips in a gesture of puzzlement. "Er, well... He's gotten jolly fast... Tobias did say Beauty is his muse." And then, catching the eye of his mother at the tea urn table, the young actor bowed. "Forgive me, duty calls."

Ting ting ting

Ella turned towards the fireplace where Sebastian the mayor now stood, a crystal glass of wine in one hand and a cream cake or something in the other. "If I may have your attention please, ladies and gentlemen..." the elderly man wheezed.

The polite conversation fell away as people found a comfortable position to sit or stand. Doctor Hyde and Gwen Pendragon extracted themselves from the centre of attention at the fireplace, leaving the mayor and Merlin in pride of place. Doctor Hyde stood to Ella's left and bowed a quick greeting. Gwen stood behind her to the right and leaned against the wall, lifting one of her sharply booted heels hard against the wallpaper. Ella felt herself wincing along with Spalding's mother at the tea urn.

The mayor gestured to Merlin with his wineglass. "It has been too long since Charmington has hosted *proper* magicians..." He half-bowed to Merlin, who slapped the old mayor's shoulder in a *you-flatter-me-you old-rogue!* gesture. Ella just held her tongue and listened through a waffly toast punctuated by Doctor Hyde snorting with disdain every time Sebastian repeated the word *exemplary*.

Ella's eyelids drooped in the warm atmosphere, and she wished she had chosen a place to sit rather than stand as she leaned heavily on her walking stick.

"And so, it was with much enthusiasm that I accepted Merlin's offer!" Sebastian mumbled, waving his cake around like a conductor with a baton. Merlin did a sharp double-take. Ella stood straighter and the wider audience likewise stretched from their slump, as obvious panic danced across Merlin's features. "A grand school with a grandmaster!" the mayor jabbered on, as if everyone had not stopped paying attention the moment he started adding 'Back in my day' in every sentence.

"Actually, Sebs, hold on there," Merlin uttered with a strained laugh as he tried to divert whatever rambling path Sebastian was on before they both reached the cliff. "It was a *theoretical* discussion, after all. More what you might call a thought experiment."

The major stuffed the last bite of cake into his mouth so he could pat Merlin's broad shoulder, while raising his glass and muttering, "Nonsense, nonsense. It is an exemplary idea."

Ella tightened her grip on the walking stick head as the mayor finally got to his point. "Raise a glass with me..." the major said to the now rapt audience "...as we toast the founding of the next prestigious school of magic, a school to rival that of Avalon! And headed by none other than our own great—nay—*magnificent*, Merlin!"

"Magnificent Merlin!" Doctor Hyde scoffed from Ella's side as everyone else raised their glasses and drank a toast to Merlin, who had turned white as a sheet.

"What is Merlin planning?" Gwen all but hissed. "He can't leave Avalon. We have a contract!" And she marched over as well-wishers swamped the pair, congratulating the jovial major and the very confused man of the hour, who now looked more like a man on the spot.

Ella tutted to herself as conversations resumed and she turned away. Whatever did Merlin think he was up to? Opening a school of magic in Charmington? Sibylla would have a word or two to say about that, most probably, 'No!' and 'No!' He could jolly well sort it out for himself. It wasn't her business...

A milling person nudged Ella. Marge the midwife. Her blond curls bounced as she placed her hands on her hips and glared. "Did you see? The mayor has eaten two slices of the *dry* coconut cake Sally bought and didn't touch my delicious homemade butterscotch macarons." The little midwife gestured to the buffet table and scooped up a plate of biscuits, which she held in front of Ella, gesturing for her to take one. "Sometimes I don't know why I bother," Marge continued, casting narrowed eyed appraisal over at the offending tray. "Store bought cake!"

Ella selected a brown macaron. She was rather fond of butterscotch. "Sally has rather a lot on her mind. It's a wonder she's here at all."

To which, Marge snarkily replied, "Huh! The mayor is probably feeling guilty for siding with Millie over the tenancy renewal of their haberdashery. Everyone knew Sally was going to be pushed out. Of course, that was yesterday! How swiftly Sally's fortunes have changed! Some people have all the luck."

Come to think of it, Marge had a point. Sally's fortunes *had* improved with the sudden death of her sister...

Ella found her eyes following Marge's towards where Sally sat forlornly on one end of the chaise lounge under the bay window overlooking the tree-lined avenue. But at that moment, Ella caught sight of Merlin hurriedly exiting out through the service door to the kitchens, chasing after a rather upset Gwen.

Magic preserve! Ella's chance to get her hands on the threatening letter was literally escaping out the door!

"Excuse me," Ella told the midwife. Still clutching the butterscotch macaron in one hand, walking stick in the other, Ella limped across the thick Persian carpet towards the swinging kitchen door, when a ruddy-faced buxom woman suddenly stepped in front of her and blocked the way. Mistress Fairweather, the orphanage matron. The woman whom Sally had asked Ella to be a character reference for only yesterday to help smooth the adoption application of her young ward, Olly.

"Sign the petition to reinstate the fairy lights?" Mistress Fairweather said, waving a clipboard under Ella's nose whilst bouncing a babe in the crook of an arm. "A well lit street means a safer Charmington for all."

"Off with you!" intervened a wheezing male voice. Sebastian, the mayor. Sidling up beside Ella, the tottering mayor snapped back at the matron, "A well-lit street only aids your thieving brats to better see what they're taking! Her Highness has no time for your petition!"

"I beg to disagree," Ella said, making a grab for the clipboard just as the matron drew herself up to her full height and, slapping the clipboard and baby to the protection of her quivering bosom, Mistress Fairweather spun away on her heel, flinging daggers of resentment at both Ella and the mayor.

"*Magic preserve!*" Ella growled under her breath and cast a look of undiluted anger at the interfering mayor. He had just ruined her chance to make a favourable impression and aid Sally's adoption of Olly! She raised a bony finger to scold the irritating senior.

Sebastian clasped his throat. With a strangled cry, the mayor collapsed. His foot kicking out caught Ella's walking stick, and she tumbled down as well, falling across the choking elderly man.

Ella untangled herself when, in a gust of carbolic soap, Doctor Hyde swooped down and was beside her on his hands and knees. The doctor swiftly loosened the mayor's cravat and pressed his ear to the old man's chest. Then he frowned and appeared to sniff the air.

Next, the Doctor grasped the mayor's limp hand, inspected his fingernails and then cautiously leaned in to sniff them as well. Doctor Hyde's cool expression of methodical calm changed instantly to abject horror, and he sat back and shouted up to the gawking onlookers. "Poison! This man has been poisoned!"

CHAPTER 14

MERLIN'S SECRET

MAYOR'S RESIDENCE, EAST AVENUE, UPPER East Side Charmington.

"Drop what you're eating!" Doctor Hyde bellowed. "The food or drink may contain poison!"

Shrieks rippled across the room and several ladies fainted as a pitter-patter of small cakes and pastries rained down onto the immaculate Persian carpet.

"Poisoned? Can you be sure?" Ella uttered as the Doctor peered closely at the old man's pupils.

"Last night someone broke into my office and stole my typewriter," Doctor Hyde whispered over his shoulder while proceeding with his medical examination of the crumpled mayor, checking teeth and gums. "I assumed it was merely youthful hijinks...but now...I think the theft was a diversion."

Once on his feet, Hyde assisted Ella to hers, placing her walking stick into her hands, and he whispered, "I must go check that my leeches and safe of poisons have not been compromised." Regret plastered across his features, he bowed and then darted off through the chaos, and the reeling mayoral family closed in about their fallen patriarch.

"Merlin!" Ella tottered a few steps back and accidentally trod on her dropped macaron. "Where is Merlin?" Could her brother's magic have averted this tragedy? Ella cast her gaze here and there, searching the confused litany of faces in the crowd. Was Merlin still in the kitchen? Ella limped away from the disintegrating social gathering and slapped her hand to the swinging service door to the household's busy kitchen.

ELLA FINALLY LOCATED GWEN AND Merlin outside in the back garden under the winter-stripped cherry trees, arguing over the mayor's announcement. The words, "I categorically deny that I'm leaving Avalon, or am setting up a private school!" ushered from Merlin's lips as Ella approached. "Why would I? I hate children! Everyone knows it!" Her brother placed a placating hand on his publisher's shoulder, but Gwen shrugged it off with a flounce of her pearls and blonde tousled hair. "C'mon, Gwen...Gwenny, you know you're my number one! My true love."

"What about what's-her-face?" Gwen muttered sourly, arms folded tightly across her red jacket, all elbows and angles. "That old woman wearing too much lace—wasn't she supposedly your one true love? I hear people talking. Maybe you came here to rekindle that love..."

Merlin touched his breastbone, imploring. "That was ages ago— fifty years—a lifetime. I told you old Sebs is daft! That conversation about setting up a school he referred to happened decades ago! He's a silly old fool."

"He's a dead old fool, I'm afraid," Ella interrupted, limping over.

Merlin and Gwen jumped back from their close proximity, like a guilty young couple many years their junior. "What? What happened?" Merlin said, clearly baffled. "How dead is Seb?"

"Completely dead," Ella answered, gesturing back to the mayoral household. "He ate a poisoned macaron or something. Do you have any spells for that?"

"Spells?" Merlin paled and swallowed. He grasped at the strap of a leather satchel slung across his shoulder. "Nuh... I don't have any spells...no spells."

"What? A poisoned macaron?" Gwen clutched her cheeks and then suddenly squeezed Merlin's face between her palms. "Oh, Merly! I nearly gave *you* a macaron. This funny little lady kept trying to make me take one! I could have killed you!" Pearls and jewels glinting, she spun about on her wickedly sharp boot heels and ran back toward the house, muttering, "This is going to be a PR nightmare!"

"It might not have been the macaron!" Ella felt compelled to add as Gwen ran off. "I was just saying... Ugh. Never mind."

With the satchel hugged to his chest like a shield, Merlin slumped down upon the wrought-iron bench seat. "Sebs is dead...no spells...could have been me..."

Ella stomped a foot. "Oh, get over yourself, *Merly*! A man is dead— admittedly a very elderly man—but a man just the same! This isn't about you! You have always had such a narcissistic streak!"

Merlin's head snapped up, and he combed his hand through his tousled roguish hair. "Hey! C'mon, sis! I've told you before, healing is not my game! You can't blame me because old Sebs can't hold his macaron!" He hunched over the brown satchel again.

"Why do you keep doing that? What have you got in there?" Ella asked as Merlin clamped about the satchel, cradling it in his arms. "Are you hiding something?"

Merlin batted her hand away. "No, I am not hiding something—this has nothing to do with you. It's just a copy of my next book, okay? A work in progress. Someone went through my stuff last night, so I didn't want to leave my notes unattended."

Ella squinted, perplexed. "Why would anyone want to steal your notes for yet another dull encyclopaedia?"

"It's not dull!" Merlin snapped, wrapping himself about the satchel. "It's gold, pure gold, I tell you! I told you I'm working on something big and this is it. It's like cracking the method of turning lead into gold! Any day now, this manuscript is going to be worth a fortune!"

Ella rolled her eyes. "Turn lead into gold! Merlin, for magic's sake. I actually thought you might be onto something for a moment." Tapping her cane on the ground for emphasis, she added, "Something to help our kingdom in its hour of financial need. But no, you're as useless as Sibylla. Why I expected anything else, I will never know!"

"Go away if you're going to be mean," Merlin sulked from his curled position on the bench. "I've got a lot on my mind. My girlfriend is dead. Someone is blackmailing me! I don't need your problems right now."

Ella did a double take. "What did you say? Your girlfriend is dead?" Ella hitched her thumb back to where Gwen had strode off. "But I thought...er...?"

"Not Gwen. My *old* girlfriend. The one I should have married!" Merlin backhanded a tear. "Oh, Ella! How can you be so heartless?" He leaned back and whined, "As if I don't have enough problems? I've lost all my magic and—and—someone is blackmailing me!"

"You've lost your magical powers?" Ella questioned. "Are you sure?"

"Yes, I'm sure!" Merlin sobbed. "It's so unfair. I'm going to be old and useless like you!"

For a moment, Ella was completely struck dumb. Then, drawing on centuries of stoic resolve, she placed a sisterly hand on her brother's shoulder. "How about we go have a quiet drink at the Huntsman Tavern, and you can tell me all about it?"

CHAPTER 15

THE HUNTSMAN TAVERN GETS AN UPGRADE

HUNTSMAN TAVERN, SOUTHGATE SQUARE, CHARMINGTON.

Ella pushed the heavy tavern door open and blinked in the gloom as her eyes adjusted to the low light. Looking back over her shoulder, she sighed, pushed the door open again, grabbed her sullen brother by his jacket lapel and dragged him into the tavern's dark interior.

With him in front of her, Ella shunted Merlin towards the bar. The Huntsman tavern appeared deserted, which wasn't unexpected because it was late afternoon. Brother and sister's features reflected off of the various bottles lining the many shelves as they approached the bar.

"Haven't been here for years. Nothing's changed..." Merlin murmured, then suddenly drew up short and Ella peered around to him to see a rather strange set up in front of the bar. The line of stools was gone and in their place, two tall tufted wingback bench seats faced each other, with a broad table between them. "I take that back. A booth? In the middle of the bar?"

"*Ja!*" snapped a child's voice and a small blonde girl, whose outward appearances suggested she was about eight years old, popped up from behind the bar and slapped a crate of bottles on the bar top, then wiped her hands on her denim dirndl skirt. "Is all zee rage in Nottingham. Sophisticated, *ja?*"

Merlin scratched his head. "Gretel, typically they line a row of private booths along the *outer* edges of the room, not front and centre," he mumbled but then shrugged, and slipped off his book bag, thumped it on the booth table and slid onto the winged back bench seat.

Gretel flicked a cloth across the surface of the new booth. "But zen I have to valk all zee way to edge. Bringing you to zee bar, save time, *ja?*" She grabbed Merlin's elbow, and with casualness borne of someone with inhuman strength, yanked him sideways so she could reach up and flatten out his dark curls. "Merlin, look at you! Nearly all grown up! How is zee big city?"

"Ow! Gretel! Stop! My hair!" Merlin batted her playful rough-housing away and flipped his hairdo back into its state of unkemptness. "And the big city is horrid. Positively horrid."

Gretel clicked her tongue as if to say she expected no less. "Vhiskey?" the little blonde vampire asked, flashing her sharp pearly canines at Ella.

"Cranberry juice, thank you," Ella said, shuffling awkwardly crablike onto the bench seat. What a strange idea these booth seats were—she didn't think they would catch on here in Charmington.

"Revivor for me," Merlin muttered, all dark looks once more, and he cradled the book bag to him and slouched over it like a pillow.

"Zat bad, is it?" Gretel muttered to herself before skipping off. "I have something special for you. Down in zee cellar."

Ella leaned her back against the tall, stiff seating. "Actually, once you're in, it's not so bad... Kind of snug. Nice and private." Craning forward, she wondered if there might be other patrons lurking in the bar. It was very dark in here, so she couldn't be sure. She tapped the fat beeswax candles that were unlit on the booth's table. "Make yourself useful and light these," she said to Merlin, and snapped her fingers in demonstration. Fingers which once could have conjured up a flame before the fairy council had bound her personal magic.

"Huh!" her brother muttered, more sourly than she expected. After a second, he reached into his jacket and drew out a little silver rectangle, which he thumbed. The boxy device split into two and a flame sparked to life. Merlin touched the flame to the wicks, then snapped the silver mechanism shut with a grumble of, "There! Happy now? Rub it in, why don't you? I told you, I have lost *all* my magic!"

Ella sat back. A bolt of comprehension hit home. "Merlin! Gracious, have the fairy council stripped *your* powers too?"

"I don't know!" her brother bawled, his grumpy exterior crumbling in with a look of pained confusion. "I don't know what's going on! Oh, magic, why have you forsaken me?"

Ella slapped her brother's elbow. "Sit up straight and pull yourself together! Think! Are you and Gwen engaged? You know Charming's forgo their magic on Wyld soil when they get engaged or marry! To prevent power struggles and discord within the ruling family line."

Merlin jolted upright and slapped his cheeks. "Oh joyous baby goats, you're right! I totally forgot that rule of magic our forefathers bound the family line to!" He looked cheerful for a second, but then appeared confused once more. "But no! I haven't asked Gwen. And the most recent Charmington person I asked to marry me was—was—Millie! Years ago!" Merlin's chin dropped to rest on his hands folded on the tabletop. "And she said *no*."

"Millie?" Ella blinked at her brother through the flicker of the candle flame. "You asked Millie? When?"

Merlin pulled the cuff of his jacket over his hand and then used it to wipe away his tears. "Decades ago..." He shut his eyes and shook his head. "Her rejection spurred me to leave here for Avalon..."

"That was fifty years ago," Ella said to herself, thinking back to that time. "Millie would have been, what, twenty-five? Twenty-seven?" She shook off the memories. "Is that why you seized on that offer from Arthur Pendragon when he came to you with that bizarre scheme of his to claim the throne involving rocks and swords?"

Merlin sat up and flicked his little flame lighting device open and shut. "It wasn't rocks and swords, don't be absurd—it was *one* rock and *one* sword, thank you very much! And it worked!" He drew the book satchel closer. "Just like this is going to work..."

"But wait!" Ella talked over the nonsense Merlin had spouted. "That doesn't make sense. Everyone knows that *you* broke Millie's heart. I assumed because you *didn't* ask her to marry you! Sally mentioned something about it just yesterday."

"I think I jolly well remember who I did, and who I didn't ask to marry me!" Merlin started listing names and counting on his fingers. "Let's see, there was Hildebrand, gosh, she was magnificent, and that lovely English Lizzie—or was Jane? She was a writer too. You know, she never married? Several Catherines—admittedly, that was confusing, but anyway, it's not even a baker's dozen!"

Ella rolled her eyes. "You are the worst! I have said it before, and I will say it again!"

Gretel saved Merlin from further scolding as the little girl rolled in, literally, on a pair of roller-skates, and plonked two clean tumblers and a dusty one hundred-year-old bottle of Mossfern whiskey on the table.

"Century old Mossfern! That's the good stuff!" Merlin said, seizing the ancient bottle and thumbing the cork free. "Gretel, my sweet angel! You were always my favourite!"

Gretel flicked a pigtail over her shoulder like a salute. "*Ja.* You are good *kinder*. Is nice catch up, but I must make zee stagecoach ready

for sunset at six. Customer is paying triple for urgent trip to Avalon."
She rolled off, followed shortly by a crash of glass, and a weary,
"Skates on is not making work faster!"

After the noises of Gretel extracting herself from the mess had
died down and Merlin had poured them both a measure of the one
hundred-year-old amber Mossfern whiskey, Ella took a sip. "I need to
see that letter for Millie, which Sally gave you yesterday."

Merlin set his whiskey down, his brow pinched. "What letter?"

Ella arched an eyebrow. "The threatening one. You know, about
bringing the *Red Hoodie* whatever manuscript to meet someone?"

Merlin's eyes went wide, and he clenched the bookbag to his chest.
"How do you know about the *Red* manuscript?"

"How do *you*? Wait?" Ella grabbed the satchel and pulled it
towards her. "Do you have the *Red* manuscript in this bag?"

Merlin lurched out to grab it back and tried to pry her fingers off,
shouting, "Stop! Let go! I must have misheard—I know nothing about
this *Cinderella* sequel!"

Ella kept on tugging. "You do! Give it to me!"

"No! No! No!" her brother cried. "It's mine. You can't tell anyone—
you can't tell Gwen!"

Ella suddenly released the bag and stood up, blinking in the half
light. Worlds colliding, she smacked her palm to the table. "Merlin!
You toad! You did it, didn't you? *You* are the anonymous author who
wrote Cinderella!"

CHAPTER 16

WHAT THE LETTER SAID

"Shush!" Merlin swept the book bag close and hugged it to his person. Furtively casting his terrified gaze into the gloom of the tavern's empty common room, he blinked up at Ella. "No one can find that out! My reputation depends on it! If anyone in the encyclopaedia circuit found out I wrote such lurid fiction, I'd be a laughingstock!"

"That may be a dent to your pride," Ella scoffed, "but you're acting as if your life were on the line."

"Ha! If *only* it were that simple!" Merlin poured a shot of whiskey and downed the amber liquid in one gulp. "Do you know how many schools have put in orders for *Merlin's Magic for Beginners* textbooks? The numbers are boggling. But no school of magic will want to touch academic references written by me if they learn about my romance side-hustle. If Gwen finds out, I can kiss my textbook contract goodbye."

"So it *could* ruin you. Just as Claude said. Hmm..." Ella tapped her fingernails on the polished wooden surface. "Why did you even bother writing *Cinderella* then, if it's such a risk to your career?"

Merlin baulked. "What? Are you mad? A tale of true love, unbridled passion and betrayal? How could I *not* write it? You just don't understand, you're not an artist. You've always had no imagination. You're as dull as a wooden spoon." He snorted and then fished a pencil out from his pocket. "That's good, I should write that down..."

Ella rolled her eyes. "Insults to my character aside. Clearly, there are people who *do* know your secret identity. Claude from the bookshop for one, and Millie, I assume. Did Millie know you wrote the *Red* manuscript?"

"Yes, but she was sworn to secrecy. And I only gave Millie the *Red* manuscript to read because I needed her to fact check details as it's loosely based on the local Charmington outlaw. You know, that hooded fellow who wore the red cape? But this new story—it's the tale of Cinderella's daughter, it follows on from when the rebellion forms and—"

"Stop! I don't want to hear it," Ella said, interrupting. "I have no interest in your lurid misrepresentation of Charmington outlaws. Magic preserve, Merlin! How can you take tragic events from our own family and turn that into a romance novel?" Ella took a moment to compose herself. "Putting your disrespect of the past to one side. Do you, or do you *not* have the note that Sally gave you last night?"

Merlin shrugged. "I have it." He extracted a piece of notepaper from in the side pocket on the book satchel. "Here. see."

Someone had ripped the top of the page off, but the body of the typed note remained, and read:

```
I know your Secret.
Get the Red Riding HooD manuscrIpt to mE.
Or everyonE fInDs out.
```

Ella frowned. "Tell me what happened. What exactly did Sally say when she gave you this?"

Merlin swept his hair back from his eyes. "I went there last night to offer my condolences. I admit I was out of sorts—my history with Millie was at the forefront of my mind."

Ella gestured to the note. "And you told Sally you could use your magic to figure out who sent this threat to the haberdashery?"

Merlin tilted his head. A guilty expression crossed his boyish features. "I did...although, truth be told, it doesn't require magic. I just said that to get out of there. Gosh, that old haberdashery brought back some memories." He shook off the thought. "I admit it was a crummy move, and I've felt like a wretch about it all morning—but seeing the note freaked me out. An obsessed fan has been harassing me," he explained. "It started a couple of months ago. They threatened if I didn't come clean, they'd expose my secret identity! And whoever sent this note to the haberdashery, it's the same rogue that has been threatening me in Avalon." He sighed and fished out from his book bag side pocket several similar typewritten notes. "I thought with this world book tour and coming here to Charmington, I'd have a reprieve from this lunatic..."

Ella sat down and spread the pages flat on the table so she could compare two side by side.

One said:

`I will tell your Secret worlD wIdE.`

The other one she chose said:

`I know your Secret ` ~~`DIE`~~ ` IDEntity.`

"While the style is undeniably similar..." Ella observed the page size and rubbed the paper between her fingers. "The paper is the same size, colour and feel. But there's no conclusive way to tell if the same individual typed the one Sally gave you."

Merlin held up a finger. "Actually, there is..." He dug around in the satchel pocket again and drew out a magnifying glass. "Look closely, examine the capital S in each note. Do you see the commonality? It's a tiny fraction higher than the other letters. Do you see?"

Ella squinted through the glass lens, holding it over the black typed letter. "I confess I cannot perceive it."

"Trust me, it's there! I've stared at these letters a lot!" Merlin nodded emphatically. "These were all typed by the same person!"

"If you say so..." Ella narrowed her eyes. Typical. He called her boring and without imagination and yet here he was foolishly jumping to conclusions because of his over indulgent imagination.

"What do you mean, *if I say so*?" Merlin pouted, hands on hips. "The indisputable proof is there in black and white!"

Ella huffed out a breath. "Indisputable... Quite so, as Doctor Hyde would say, observe, what is indisputable? If I concede your observation about the typewriter keys, and while the writing *style* is eerily similar. We can *only* conclude that these notes were typed on the *same machine*—not necessarily by the same *person. Ha!* I think the plain, boring facts rather overrule your lurid flights of imagination there, don't you?"

Merlin opened his mouth as if to argue, but then closed it, stood up, and pounded a fist on to the table. "Edison..." he muttered to himself. "Edison *indisputable* Hyde! Of course! It makes sense now— Hyde's always been wildly jealous of my success! He would love to see me ruined!" Merlin swept up the notes and stuffed them in his bag. "I will take care of this! Thank you for your help, sis!"

Ella blanched as her brother hurriedly stuffed the pages back into the bookbag. "Merlin! Magic preserve, you old fool—you can't think

Doctor Hyde is blackmailing you! If *even* Gwen doesn't know you wrote *Cinderella*, how could Hyde?" She grabbed the bag just as Merlin stood. The main clasp sprang open and manuscript pages spilled out across the booth table.

"Curse it all!" Merlin growled, slapping at Ella's hands as she helped sweep the pages together. "Keep your hands off my novel!" Glancing at the pages, the colour suddenly drained from his face. He upended the bag and dumped out the remaining pages. "No! No! No!" Frantically, Merlin scoured the manuscript. "It's not here!"

"What are you talking about?" Ella demanded as paper rained onto the floorboards.

Merlin balled several pages into his fists and waved them under her nose. "This *isn't* the *Red Riding Hood* manuscript!" he rasped. "It's a fake! A dummy! *Red Riding Hood* has been stolen!"

CHAPTER 17

WULF

"A fake?" Ella picked up a page at random and started reading.

But it was only the word 'bosom' repeated over and over, filling the entire page.

"Are you sure? It reads like your dross."

"I know my own story!" Merlin growled. The satchel strap flung over his shoulder, he sprinted for the door.

Ella trailed in his wake, the fake manuscript page clutched in her hand. "Are you just leaving this mess? Merlin, get back here!"

Though she reached the tavern door a minute behind her brother, there was no sign of Merlin when Ella ventured out into daylight. She stood blinking in the sunlight on the tavern's porch and squinted at the neighbouring buildings nestled within Southgate Square.

Perhaps Merlin had darted across to the bakery? Or maybe Bron the baker had at least seen which way her brother went?

Ella stuffed the fake manuscript page in her skirt pocket. She then trekked the short distance over the cobbles to the neighbouring building and tapped her cane against the door, which opened at that very moment.

Baker Bron, carrying a willow basket of sourdough loaves, gasped and dropped the basket. "You!" he uttered, backpedalling into the bakery. "No!" The door slammed shut, the baker abandoning his bouncing bread to the bakery porch.

Magic preserve! What was wrong with the fellow?

Ella banged her cane head against the stout wooden door as she eyed the sourdough rolls spread out on the slats of the porch. What a waste. "Open up! Whatever is the matter?"

"No! Go away! I can't take it!" cried the distraught voice of Bron the baker behind the door, over the scrape and thump of something heavy being hauled against the door. "For the love of sweet mercy! I'll not be called a murderer or werewolf *this* month!"

"It's nothing of the sort. I just thought you might have seen which way Merlin went," Ella answered, stepping back from the door. She peered through the bakery window, but a curtain was yanked across her vision. "Come on, man! Don't be such a coward!"

"Go away! Please leave me in peace—can't I have one month when no one tries to hang me or lock me up?"

"Oh! Don't exaggerate!" As if she had accused him of anything *last* month? Had she...? No! Grumbling to herself, Ella backed away and stepped off the bakery porch and went in search of Merlin.

Her mind in a whirl, and feeling every year of her centuries long life, Ella walked as best she could along the cobbles. If Merlin were so pig-headed as to go accusing Doctor Hyde of being his blackmailer, then, most likely, he would head straight to the hospital in the industrial area of Hot Cockle Lane.

After checking her bearings, Ella ventured down a narrow alleyway that should prove a handy shortcut between buildings and get her there faster. Hopefully, before Merlin made a fool of himself or did anything embarrassing that would ruin any chance of Ella cementing her friendship with the good doctor. Hyde was a sensible fellow, but surely there was a limit to the number of embarrassing relatives that even a man of science would ignore.

Lost in her thoughts, Ella didn't see the tall graceful figure peeling from the shadows of the stables at the back of the Huntsman Tavern and slipping like a keen knife in the dark after her...

"Should have known," Ella mumbled to herself, eyes intent on every footstep as the darkened nature of the alley between the looming buildings blunted her eyesight. The cobbles underfoot were more slippery and coated with slime from lack of sunlight or frequent foot traffic. "Merlin embarrasses me every time he shows up..."

Taking a moment to stretch her back, she heard the tread of a footfall one step behind. One step and no more... As if someone was trying to walk and match her footsteps... Gripping the cane, Ella carried on her way and listened intently. Had she imagined it? Should she turn around, or...?

"Aha!" Ella cried, spinning around, her cane clasped high. She smacked the tall man behind her square in the chest. He did not flinch. Face obscured by a black felt hood, only his neatly trimmed beard was visible.

The hood swept back, and he quirked an eyebrow. A shock of white hair stood out above his right eye in an otherwise smooth pelt of inky black.

"Silver?" he intoned, eyeing the head of the cane now pressed to his heart. "And I thought we were friends?"

"Wulf!" Ella sagged, withdrawing the cane she slouched over it. "Magic preserve! You scared the life out of me! I nearly bashed your head in!"

Prince John's bodyguard's lips twitched, and he touched a hand to his breastbone as if thinking of a suitable response. He blinked. "Ouch. That will bruise."

"Oh, don't mock me! Fine! I'm glad you're not hurt," Ella snapped, still a little shaken. "You shouldn't sneak up on people!"

Wulf bowed, remembering his manners. "Apologies for the stealth, my lady, it's a bad habit formed from many years of bad company. I will not forget your...lesson."

Sweeping her grey hair back, and wondering if the tall man before her was laughing at her, she claimed the high ground before she sank any lower. "See that you do not."

Ella looked over her shoulder with a sigh. Acknowledging any chance she had of catching up with Merlin before he spoke to Doctor Hyde was lost, she turned back.

Though she looked away for only a second, Wulf was now several feet away. He sat lounging on a barrel and idly picking at his fingernails with a dagger, as if he had been waiting many hours. That was odd. She seldom saw Wulf so at his ease. It was almost as if he were *acting* nonchalant.

There seemed to be a lot of acting going on today. No doubt Wulf wanted information on Robinne, but was too proud to ask. *How was she doing? Why hadn't she written back to him?* The trivial things young people had on their minds in between assassinations or whatever daring missions Prince John tasked Wulf to attend.

Ella counted down in her head. *Five. Four. Three...*

"John wants to know if you're attending his party? You haven't RSVP'd."

"Huh? Party?" Ella cocked her head. "Oh, the coronation. Probably. Haven't thought much about it. Why?"

Clad in black, one of Wulf's shoulders rose in a languid shrug, graceful like a swirl of water... Ella shook her head to clear her thoughts. There was a hypnosis magic encasing Wulf, she was sure. Why else did her logical thoughts dissolve into puddles whenever he turned up?

"Just wondering...have you chosen your plus one?"

Plus one? Ella was confused. "Oh, I see, a companion guest. Why? Do you have a suggestion?" Ella rubbed her chin and feigned thoughtfulness. "Gosh. I wonder if Robinne would be free that day? She's been so helpful to me and a young woman like that, when would she have the chance of getting out and seeing the world?"

Wulf was now stretching, standing beside the barrel, though she had not seen him rise. He unsheathed a second knife from a boot with practised ease. "Robinne has an aunt in Nottingham. I thought it might be nice for her to catch up with family..."

"How very noble of you," Ella replied, suppressing an eye roll. "Most people would recommend I bring a bodyguard, or perhaps a statesman or diplomat, but no, you suggest a pretty girl who loathes politicians and royalty."

Wulf had the good grace to grin as he continued with his limbering exercises. "What can I say? I'm a thoughtful guy. Besides, you won't need a bodyguard if I'm there, will you?"

Ella tipped her head. "But what if John decided I needed to be eliminated? Hmm?"

Wulf walked a few steps, twirling blades in each hand. "I admit, that would be...awkward."

"Are all the knife tricks necessary?" Ella said, her temper waning. "There's no need to labour the point. If you want me to bring along Robinne, just say."

"Oh no, these are not for you," Wulf said, affronted. "These are for the two chaps lurking in that doorway twenty feet beyond..."

There was a grunt, a door slam and a pounding of running feet.

Wulf cocked his head. "I guess they decided today was not a good day to die..." The knives returned to their holsters, and he offered Ella his arm. "Shall we?"

"Er...Why yes, thank you..." By accident, Ella tapped her cane twice to the cobbles which engaged the light mechanism. A golden hue flooded out in a six-foot pool from the tip of the walking stick. "Gracious, I should have thought of turning that on before! It's so gloomy here."

"Oh, your stick is an original Watson Lady's Special Companion! Do you mind?" Wulf said, dark flinty eyes enthused, and attaching Ella's hand to his elbow, he supported her so he could examine the cane as they walked. "These have a hidden stiletto dagger, didn't you know?"

"I can't remember how to free it," she admitted, embarrassed, trying to lengthen her stride so that Wulf wouldn't think she was short *and* slow.

"Grip the cane head firmly...then with your other hand, place it here, just below this silver line. That's the separation point. Place your thumb on this brass rivet, third down. Press—it's the catch release—and...twist, pull and release! There! That's a beauty! Tempered steel!" He grinned at the blade. "There's a later model where they replace the dagger with an umbrella."

"Doesn't sound as useful," Ella responded.

"My thoughts exactly," Wulf returned, happily. Slotting the blade back into the handle, he tucked the stick under his free arm and patted Ella's hand. "Anyway, where are you headed? I can escort you."

CHAPTER 18

THE CINDERELLA MEMORIAL PARK SNOW FIGHT

CINDERELLA MEMORIAL PARK – CENTRAL CHARMINGTON.

Ella and Wulf parted ways as they crested the top of Main Street. Wulf veered off towards the Mercantile arcade, a collection of businesses that nestled around the Sutherby auction house. A jaunty banner touting *Grand Magical Auction Tonight 6pm onwards!* hung across the entranceway of the auction house.

For a moment Ella reflected that the auction house was where her flying carpet was being sold off tonight—the proceeds from which were going to pay for the repair to Doctor Hyde's charity hospital. It crossed her mind that perhaps Prince John had sent Wulf to place a bid on the carpet, but then children's laughter and Willow's voice rang out and drew her attention.

Ella crossed the road intersection to stand at the railings of the Cinderella Memorial Park Garden and gawked out at the small park on the hillside below. The familiar view of park benches, the central statue of Cinderella, and the stunted shrubbery, usually bent low over a fresh dumping of snow, was transformed. Before her lay a peculiar landscape dotted with snow fortresses and castles. Snowmen, shaped to look like guards, were littered here and there, and children's bright laughing faces popped up to heft snowballs at a towering snow-castle structure with elaborate crenulations.

She heard a yip of a small dog and caught sight of Mr. Puddles, his purple tricorn askew as Dirk Turpin the coachman lifted the dog up, and at his side, Cheapcuts waved a flag of sorts made from a broom and several pairs of socks, and cried out, "Surrender or face thy doom!"

"Never!" came back a cry and giggle, and Willow and Sam's heads peeped out the top of a snow turret. They whispered to each other and pointed at something, as if debating the staging of an attack on their enemy.

"Yoo hoo! Willow!" Ella called and waved to her. The young witch waved back—the jangling of her bracelets apparently giving her position away as a barrage of snowballs flew from all angles and Willow ducked down with a shriek.

Ella flinched back as Tomcat suddenly jumped down from the head of a nearby snowman. "Haha! You didn't see me up there, did you?"

"No, indeed, white on white, you were quite disguised as a snowman's toupee," Ella muttered, wiping a trace of snow that Tom's motion had flicked on her cheeks. Oh, it was icy cold. How could all the children bear it?

The rallying cries from Dirk and Cheapcuts turned into wails of annoyance along with yips from Mr. Puddles as their fort collapsed when a surge of snow, moving in a slow wave, overwhelmed their base. Sandy, his blonde locks dripping wet, popped out of the snow-wave like a mole from its burrow, stole off with Cheapcut's sock flag and disappeared under the snow mound again, which sunk back into the landscape. Ella blinked. Goodness, that was definitely an innate display of Wyld magical power there... How interesting.

Shaking snow from her coat, Willow made her way up to the railing at the top of the park, her cheeks rosy.

Ella gestured to the moving mound of snow that gave away Sandy's position under the snow as another snowman collapsed and more children Ella was not familiar with swarmed out from various tunnels and started scooping up the snow to rebuild their walls. "Sandy is showing clear signs of elemental talent..."

Still breathless, Willow nodded, and drew out Ella's leather notebook from her colourful patchwork coat. "Gosh, yes!" She flipped open the notebook to show Ella a bunch of tasks and ticks alongside various children's names. "Several kids joined us along the way—and as soon as we started the snow fort everyone wanted to play!"

"Are any astute?" Ella asked. "Has anyone transformed the snow from its natural loose state into a solid ice state?"

Willow shook her snow damp hair as Tomcat stood up on his hind legs to lean against the railing. "What do you mean? Transform it into a solid?"

Ella held out her palm. "Imagine I held a snowball... An individual with astute raw wyld magic can transform that compacted snow into a single solid ice matrix. Sibylla was transmuting simple fallen snow into icicle rattles, or later, solid ice music boxes from a very young age."

"Ooh!" Tomcat breathed out, his little pink mouth agape, and steam curled out with his breath. "Ice music boxes? That sounds wonderful, beautiful..."

"Magical," Ella added with a nod, recalling the dazzling ice crystal structures her twin had made many human lifetimes ago now. Astutes were exceptionally rare, even among her kind. For one to appear among the general human population was unlikely...

Her thoughts drew back to the present as Willow asked, "There's something a little strange, though. Over thirty percent of children show signs of innate magic. I know Wyld Kingdom has soil enriched with powerful, ancient magic, but the numbers do seem high." She frowned at her notes. "Maybe I've measured some tasks wrong?"

Ella shrugged off the young woman's concern and clasped both hands to the railings to watch the children's play continue as a tall tower rose out of the snow and a child Ella didn't recognize popped out the top and waved down to their friends. "I'm sure you have done everything right. There are a lot of witches and fairy blood, though diluted, in these human children. The Charming family has lived in these mountains for a very long time..." She surveyed the laughing chaos, and ducked as a hail of snowballs whizzed overhead and the new snow tower toppled in a slow motion flurry of ice and snow and laughter. "And what about young Bethany? Has she joined in?"

Willow hitched a thumb at a little tea shoppe overlooking the memorial park. "She didn't want to play. She said her granny would be cross if she ruined her new mittens. Cassidy has taken her to Lottie's for hot chocolate."

"Oh, we should join them," Tomcat voiced and wrapped paws around his little body with a shudder. "I'm colder than I look, and Lottie's has a roaring open fire. It's very cosy." His whiskers fanned as he looked towards the pretty little shoppe where Bethany and Cassidy sat alongside fashionable women in the large picture window, their furs and capes draped loosely about the chairs.

"Bethany's grandmother Betty had a good spark of wyld magic as a little girl, I remember," Ella began, looking over at the tea shoppe. "Unfortunately, there was a nasty incident..." Ella swallowed grimly, recalling grabbing a horse whip off of a visiting dignitary who caught young Betty playing in the prince's carriage. "The grandmother has probably warned Bethany about the perils of revealing one's magic." Ella straightened. "Fear is a teacher too." She shook off her melancholy thoughts. "One step at a time, we will show Bethany she has nothing to fear and let her develop in her own time." Ella pointed to the memorial statue of her sister Cinderella, depicting the young woman holding a bird in her outstretched hand. "Have you tried any of the animal tests, Willow? That may peak Bethany's curiosity to have a turn. Trying to coax a sparrow to land on one's hand is something most children enjoy."

"Not yet," Willow confessed with a gesture to the snow forts. "We got rather carried away."

"No rush, all in good time," Ella returned. "All that matters is they're having fun."

"Duck!" cried Tom, flinching back from the rails. A second too late.

A snowball caught Ella square on the chin and she tumbled back into Willow's arms. "Oh, good gracious me!" Ella uttered, biting back a more colourful retort and wiping her stinging chin with as much dignity as she could muster.

The silence echoing out from the snow forts was palpable.

Seconds ticked by and then a dog barked.

"Mr. Puddles says Dirk threw that!" piped up Sam's voice from the snow-dusted shrubbery.

"Puddles, you little tattletale!" returned Dirk's voice from behind a snowman and he peered out and doffed his tricorn. "Apologies, ma'am."

Ella waved his apology off and turned her back as chaos erupted once more.

"Hot chocolate?" Tomcat suggested again.

Ella pulled her cloak tight about her shoulders. "I'm afraid I just popped by to see how things were going. If you're still happy to attend to the children, I'll leave you to it?" Ella asked, adding this last question to Willow.

"Oh, yes, I'm learning a lot. Now that I see your notes, I understand what my granny was looking for in me. I just thought it was fun at the time and I didn't even realise she was testing my abilities." Willow hunched. "Now I do though, I must have failed ninety-nine percent of the tasks... It's a wonder she didn't give up on me. I must have been a very dull student. Barely burgeoning and miles from astute."

Ella patted the young witch's arm. "Nonsense, my dear, you have a knack for herbals that have come from years of dedicated study. Did you know, I too was classified as burgeoning?"

"But you earned a wand!" Willow said, wide-eyed. "I could never dare dream!"

"Hard work and discipline earned me that wand," Ella returned determinedly, but then rather deflated, recalling what had lost it. Poor choices... Pride? She sighed. "Wyld magic may be showy, but talent alone leads nowhere. And if one can't harness the academic discipline to control wyld astute magic, what good is it?" Ella swept an arm to encompass the snow that decorated every roof and the smoking chimney pots of every picturesque building. "We have had this picture perfect winter everyday since my astute sister came to the throne. Ice is Sibylla's element, but she can't do anything else. Pretty as it is, decades of freezing cold grows thin." Ella nodded towards the tea shoppe. "Why don't you take all the children in for hot chocolate? Have it billed to the castle." She extracted the chunky chain of office from her neckline and gently looped it over Willow's head. "Here's my official unicorn seal, if they give you any trouble. See that everyone gets some supper to take home to their families as well."

Willow nodded. Placing two fingers to her mouth, she whistled sharply and then yelled, "Oy oy! Tea break, you lot, gather round!"

While Willow marshalled the children, Ella looked down at Tomcat. "Stay here if you want. I'm making my way to Hot Cockle Lane to talk to Doctor Hyde—hopefully I'm not too late and Merlin hasn't made a complete fool of himself."

"I'm with you, of course," Tomcat said, throwing a regretful glance towards the picture window where Bethany and Cassidy sat. "I promised to help..." He padded alongside as Ella tapped her cane along the street and waved a final farewell to Willow and the children, who teamed around the young woman as she counted heads. There were at least a dozen children swelling the ranks now.

"Gosh, to be young again," Ella muttered wistfully to herself as the children marched across the street, all lined in pairs, the older ones helping the small, Mr. Puddles frisking and leaping at their sides. Dirk saluted Ella, hoisted the sock flag over his shoulder while Cheapcuts and the others rang out an old army tune Dirk must have taught them for their game *'An army marches on its feet! But the Quartermaster averts true disaster, and supper is the answer to all peace!'*

"Did you catch up with Merlin?" Tomcat asked, falling in step, his tail swishing left and right to the beat of the children's song fading in the distance. "I followed Claude, and he took his letter to the queen's castle."

Ella narrowed her eyes. "Ah, is that because he knew Merlin was staying there? Interesting... We shall have to follow up."

"Why would Claude want to give Merlin the letter?" Tom's right ear perked up. "Oh, because his entourage are from Avalon? Will they return home before the postage barge?"

"No, because Merlin *is* the author of *Cinderella*," Ella said quietly.

"What?" Tomcat stopped dead in his tracks and had to catch up to Ella a second later. "Oh, my gosh! Merlin's *so* talented! Is there anything he can't write?"

Ella held her tongue.

"What about the threatening letter Millie was sent? Were you able to read it? Were there any clues?"

"Yes, to add to our problems. It would appear that the letter writer who threatened Millie is also sending my brother blackmail."

Tom's ears dipped and twitched. After a minute of thought, he said, "It's kinda strange Merlin's blackmailer would write to Millie as well... Maybe they knew one of them wrote *Cinderella* but wasn't sure who, and so thought they'd target both Millie and Merlin to hedge their bets?"

Ella gripped her walking stick. "That could well be."

"Wait, hold on, that means the blackmailer *must also be* a resident of Charmington?"

Ella tapped her Watson's Lady's Special Companion to the hard cobblestones. "Precisely."

"But why would this blackmailer kill Millie? Even if they thought she was the author of *Cinderella*?" Tom's tail flicked across the cobbles. "Surely blackmail only works if the target is alive?"

"Target..." Ella leaned on her walking stick and stared into space for a moment, replaying the day's events through her mind. "Hedge their bets... A case of mistaken identity...?"

The writers' walk, which collapsed, had been built for Merlin... Merlin had been standing next to the mayor not long before he was poisoned...

What if Millie and the mayor hadn't been the intended targets?

Assuming the blackmailer now had the sought after *Red* manuscript in their possession, did they need her brother alive?

CHAPTER 19

CUTTHROAT GWEN

"You see, Merlin narrowly escaped being poisoned at the mayor's afternoon tea," Ella explained to Tomcat as they walked down Main Street, heading towards riverside where the charity hospital was located in the warehouse district. "I am mulling on a theory that our villain is someone who has a motive solely against Merlin. Whether they stole the Red manuscript for ruining Merlin's reputation by exposing him, or even to keep it for themselves, matters not. Merlin, and not Millie, could have also been the true target of the writers' walk collapse. Tie up any loose threads, you see?"

"Oh! Yes—the display was built in his honour after all," Tomcat agreed as they trotted along the slight slope of the road. "Do you know anyone who has a grudge against Merlin?"

Ella rolled her eyes. "Where to begin? Merlin antagonises fellows and breaks female hearts wherever he goes. A list of friends would be shorter..."

"Claude is his friend. He said so himself."

"Perhaps Claude has poorer taste than I realised," Ella said.

Tomcat suddenly sat in the middle of the path, his tail upright like a flagpole. "Ella! Poison! The mayor was poisoned and Doctor Hyde is a poison expert—he wrote the book! Does Doctor Hyde have a grudge against Merlin?"

Ella thought back to the humiliation Merlin had dished out the day before, belittling the good doctor's poor book sales. "Er...no...? No! The doctor was the one who identified the poison! He'd hardly do that if he were guilty, would he?"

"Oh, Ella, look there! Back the way we've come!" Tomcat said, pointing behind Ella to the corner of Fifth Street in the distance. "There's Claude! Go grab him. Quiz him for known enemies of Merlin!"

Ella glanced at the person, wearing a hooded emerald green cloak, as they disappeared around the corner of the antiques shop. "Are you sure that's Claude?"

"I followed him before—it's the same cloak—it has to be him!" Tomcat darted off but had to stop and wait for Ella to catch up.

Puffing, Ella reached the corner and came up short, as an angry male voice ranted, "False beauty! You hide behind lies when you should reveal the truth!"

The emerald cloaked figure stood berating Gwen Pendragon, who looked unamused.

"Claude?" Ella said, shocked. But the voice didn't sound like Claude.

The cloaked person glanced back, then shouldered past Gwen, who just rolled her eyes and strolled down past the antique shop's stack of crates to where Ella and Tomcat stood on Main Street.

Ella exchanged glances with Tomcat, who nodded in silent understanding and followed the awful man.

"Are you all right, my dear?" Ella cried, dismayed, as the cloaked person stormed out of sight over the crest of the street curve with Tomcat's lithe white shape a short distance behind. "Who was that ungallant man?"

Gwen straightened her red leather jacket, jingling her pearls and gold chains. "Just some random nut job." She hitched a thumb at the winding little alley off Fifth Street. "If you're looking for Clod, he's in his tiny shop preparing for Merlin's book signing at six."

"Clod?" Ella blanched. Had she heard the young lady right?

Gwen shook her blonde tousled hair dismissively. "I never would have offered a premier signing if Merly had told me what a non-event Clod's store is." She examined her brightly painted red fingernails. "You wouldn't get this amateur BS in Nottingham... Catch you later." Waving farewell, she trekked off, her sharp-heeled boots ringing out against the cobbles like whip cracks.

How rude. Fancy calling charming Claude a clod and dismissing his quaint bookshop! When he spoke nothing but kindness about Merlin's appalling books. No wonder Gwen was Merlin's girlfriend! She was just as bad as him. They were a perfect match.

Ella tutted to herself as her cane tapped along the cobbles. What would such a woman do if she learned Merlin had lost his magic powers?

And if Merlin's academic reputation *was* ruined with the revelation of his romance writing side hustle, would Gwen cut her losses and get rid of the big useless lump?

Magic preserve. Who would have thought such a pretty girl would be such a cutthroat type?

CHAPTER 20

HIDING IN PLAIN SIGHT

INTERSECTION FIFTH AND MAIN STREET, EAST-CENTRAL CHARMINGTON.

"Lost him!" Tomcat's annoyed voice broke into Ella's thoughts several minutes later as she waited on the street, sheltering from the wind in the lee of a doorway. "There was a mean dog blocking my way," Tom said. "I couldn't get past. The guy wasn't Claude though—I saw Claude in his shop as I went by."

"I gathered as much from the lack of a French accent... But in the meantime, I've been thinking. Merlin said he's been receiving threats for a couple of months." Ella drew out the fake manuscript page from her pocket. "And someone went to the trouble of making a phoney manuscript to swap for the real one ahead of time. But despite their careful planning, this page from their bizarre fake may be their undoing. Leaving evidence behind..."

"But one typewritten document looks much like another," Tom pointed out. "Surely that's the point? As Sally pointed out, it's the perfect way to disguise handwriting."

"Agreed. But whether or not the blackmailer is aware of it, we *can* identify the individual machine they typed this page with." Merlin had shown her proof of that with his magnifying glass. "Not that I fancy having to inspect samples from every infernal contraption in town. Where would we even start?"

"Oh! I have it!" Tomcat gasped and covered his paw over his mouth. "What if the blackmailer *loaned* their typewriter to Sally for the writers' walk display?"

"Interesting... While strung up over the archway *none* of the machines could be used," Ella said thoughtfully. "The display itself is the perfect hiding place—hiding in plain sight."

"Yes, and what if this person who loaned Sally a typewriter was afraid they would fall under suspicion? Or what if they simply needed to type more threats? More blackmail? What if their *urgent need* to get their typewriter *back* accidentally caused the display to collapse in the first place?"

"But surely any old typewriter would serve their immediate blackmailing purposes?" Ella said. "What could be so *special* about a single typewriter?" Ella shook her head. "Like you said, they're *not* magic. And they may be expensive, but they are plentiful. You just have to know where to look."

"Good point... Ah! Of course! That could explain the theft of Tobias' machine!" Tom's bright emerald eyes lit up. "Lots of people know he writes novels! And maybe while stealing the poison from Hyde, it occurred that if they *also* stole the doctor's typewriter, then people would notice the *peculiar* theft of typewriters as the pattern and *not* even realise they had also stolen the poison?"

Ella nodded, agreeing with Tom's clever deductions. She shivered and drew her woollen cloak tight as a chilly mountain breeze swirled down the cobbled street. All this standing around outside in the cold was not doing her old bones any favours.

"They couldn't know that Hyde would be at the mayor's afternoon tea and so quick to reveal their method!" Tomcat added. Though the breeze swirled through his coat, seemingly, the cold did not trouble him. But then again, with his cat's fur coat, why would it?

"Agreed. And if the blackmailer *knew* that Merlin and Hyde have a rivalry, perhaps they even assumed that Hyde would not attend the afternoon tea!" Ella rubbed her temples. Was there anyone she knew of that was aware of Merlin and Hyde's rivalry, other than Merlin or Hyde themselves? Drat. None that she could think of.

"This is all becoming very complicated," Ella sighed. "It would be easier if one person *alone* had an obvious motive against Merlin—but being the obnoxious fellow that he is! Well. We will just have to investigate with the known facts to hand—this manuscript page."

"Yes! Let's at least start with the half dozen typewriters that fell from the display. Olly and the other children were morbidly discussing that the typewriters that killed Millie are stored in the tack room at the back of the police station stables. We can do a type test and compare it against that page you took from Merlin—although, maybe I had better do the typing," Tom suggested as they moved along. "No offence, but you were very slow."

Ella thinned her lips as they threaded their way through carriages and plodding horse-drawn carts laden with goods. "Very well then, I shall play lookout. That's probably best because if Axel spots a cat typing, I don't think even the magical amnesty will keep you safe."

"I can outrun him," Tom said with jaunty swagger to his trot. "I've done it before."

"Tom! Are you saying that Axel has chased you before? Magic preserve! What if he caught you?"

Tomcat shrugged. "Don't worry. I can look after myself. I won't get captured *this* month. Promise."

THERE WAS A LARGE COLOURFUL banner strung over the police station doorway that read, 'Magical Amnesty – hand in prohibited items NOW or Else!' and a steady stream of people entered the building.

Perhaps they thought it best to take advantage of the amnesty? Ella thought. Despite the banner's jaunty colour-scheme, the message had an underlying threatening tone... Hmm. It was no wonder the turnout of pupils for her magical lessons had been low.

"It appears our sheriff will be kept well occupied. Good," Ella muttered as she and Tomcat crept around through the side gate to the stable area at the back of the station.

At the far end of the stable block, a couple of town guards and a groom were playing dice. One groom looked up as Ella, with her walking stick in hand, tapped across the yard.

She muttered something about tax inspection. The groom shrugged, his attention quickly back to the dice, and Ella stopped and patted the horses with their heads hanging out over half doors. Once the men became engrossed back in their game, she crept down the stable block to the tack room.

The door handle turned under her grasp. The scene of leather and beeswax filled the well-kept room. Seven typewriters of various shapes and sizes sat placed neatly on a large table.

Tomcat leapt up on the table and wound through the typewriters as Ella grasped hold of one. She tipped it back and squinted underneath at a rectangle of card tied by a ribbon to the device. "Ah, excellent. This one is labelled...*Borrowed from the office of Marley, the accountant.*"

"There's no paper though," Tom pointed out as he tiptoed between the contraptions.

Ella frowned. "Drat! That didn't occur." She extracted the crumpled fake page from her pocket and turned it over. Fortunately, it was blank on the other side. "We'll use this. You type while I double-check that Sally has diligently labelled the owner's name on every machine."

Tomcat's whiskers fanned as he perched in front of the first typewriter. "What should I type?"

Ella fed the paper into the machine and avoided eye contact. "Bosom."

Tomcat arched a furry eyebrow. "Just bosom? Are you sure?" He flipped the paper hanging out the back of the heavy black model to read the original side. "Oh, I see... Bosom it is..." He sought and tapped the keys while Ella checked for labels on the six other typewriters.

"Oh, look!" Ella held up a thick card tied to a smaller model machine. "The label on this little one on the end reads Dr Hyde!"

Tomcat stopped typing. "What? But his one was stolen!" He stretched across the desk and peered at the label. "Could Doctor Hyde have *two* typewriters? Maybe this portable model is a backup? It would be useful for someone who travels a lot."

Someone who travelled a lot? Hmm, could that be true of Hyde? Ella shrugged. "You seem to know more of them than me. But you did say typewriters were expensive, so owning two seems unlikely when the hospital is short of funds."

"What about all the money you donated from selling your flying carpet?"

"The auction selling the carpet is on tonight. Until then, there is no extra money." Ella shook her head. "Besides, I can't imagine Edison would treat himself to any luxuries before resolving all the issues at the hospital. Edison Hyde is a hardworking and thoughtful man. Quite unlike my showboat of a brother. If anyone could be likely to indulge in the unnecessary purchase of extra typewriters, it would be Merlin."

Tom stopped tapping away on the keys. "Extra typewriters... Ella, look! How many typewriters are there here?"

Ella glanced around the table. "Seven? So?"

"Only one side of the writers' walk display gave way! One side means *half* of the display—six out of twelve typewriters! There should only be six here, not seven!" He prowled around, darting from one machine to the next. "One is hidden in plain sight!"

Ella baulked. "Which one? They are all labelled. I have checked." She listed the names on her fingers. "The accountant Marley, one from the haberdashery, Claude's, Marge the midwife, two from the town hall, and Hyde's."

"One is a fake?" Tomcat gulped. "A wolf in sheep's clothing!"

"Quick. Finish the test," Ella said, urging him on with the task while nodding in agreement. "Though the label might or might not be genuine, there's no denying we will have found the culprit's typewriter when the typed letters match the fake manuscript page!"

Chapter 21

The Handsome Mystery Stranger Revealed

Tack Room, Police Station Stables, Northgate Square, Charmington.

Tom resumed his seat and hit the keys. "There. First one is done! It would be quicker if you moved the paper along for me, please," Tomcat said, holding up his less dexterous cat paws. And she extracted the sheet and set up the next model over. "There's something else we haven't considered," he said as she wound the paper in. "Taking into account the all people who know Merlin's secret identity, that means we can't rule out Claude."

"We can't rule out anything or anyone until you finish testing all the machines," Ella retorted. "Offices overlook the archway. Someone could have accidentally knocked the seventh typewriter out from an office window above the walkway—possibly it was simply a theft gone wrong. That could explain why there are seven rather than six. I don't know why you'd accuse Claude. What does he actually have to gain?"

"I'm *not* accusing Claude, I'm just saying. For all we know, there could be a person out there who has a grudge we know nothing about. An old girlfriend, perhaps. A spurned lover? Merlin has a reputation as a heartbreaker... Revenge is as strong a motive as greed."

"True..." Ella tapped her toe. "So is jealousy... Gwen struck me as a jealous type, and someone capable of anything. But Merlin was adamant she didn't know his secret identity, and he's keen to keep it like that. He implied if she found out, she would break off their relationship to protect her publishing business."

"What if she *had* found out?" Tom questioned as he typed. "Recently, I mean? Maybe it spurred her to act? I imagine she'd feel deeply betrayed that he kept it from her."

Ells shook her head. "Merlin said he's been receiving threatening letters for some time."

"I'm done here," Tomcat said and moved out of the way so Ella could move the paper to the third typewriter. "Speaking of jealousy, there's something to consider. Other writers!"

"Doctor Hyde is *not* jealous of Merlin's success!" Ella snapped, scything her hand through the air. Magic preserve. Why would Tom even suggest a thing? It was as absurd as saying that she herself was jealous of Merlin's success. Ha!

"Actually, I was going to suggest Tobias because he also writes romance novels like *Cinderella*. But you have a point. Hyde *could* be jealous."

"Granted, I would have given you Tobias, except for the fact he has had a novel accepted for publication. Sally congratulated him yesterday. He was clearly very proud about it." Ella put her hands on her hips. "Since we're listing possible suspects—absurd as they may be—why not accuse Sally then, too?"

"Well...since *you* brought it up. As unorthodox as killing someone by a typewriter would be for most people, if I was a weak old woman—no offence—"

"Offence taken," Ella huffed, crossing her bony arms.

"—then dropping something heavy on someone from a height is a clever plan. As you said, they'd just have to push it off from a window ledge above. Line it up so it hits the typewriter display on the way down and creates a kind of chain reaction. No one would even think to look for an extra typewriter on the ground."

"Sally intentionally killed Millie? Is that what you're saying?" Ella drew a breath to laugh off the suggestion when another thought crossed her mind. "Could there be *two* villains afoot? One after Millie and the other after Merlin?"

Tomcat shrugged. "Merlin could still have been the target. Revenge for breaking Millie's heart all those years ago? But Millie moved into the line of sight of the dropped typewriter's path at the last second—wrong place at the wrong time?"

Ella's brow furrowed. She narrowed her eyes and hummed to herself as she contemplated various scenarios. "And Sally and Millie had a falling out last month. Would Sally set their feud aside just because the chance to get back at Merlin suddenly came her way?" Ella thought back over the previous morning. She had been at the table when Axel came along. He stirred up Sally over the sister's feud regarding the ownership of their haberdashery. Sally had thrown her glove down angrily. She stormed out, absolutely fuming at Millie...

No, in the moments leading up to Millie's death, Sally wouldn't have had Merlin's downfall on her mind... She would have had Millie's...

"But why then enlisted my help to solve the murder?" Ella wondered aloud. "Sally complimented me—us—on how we solved those dreadful goings on last month. Why would she say that?" Unless...unless Sally hadn't meant what she said.

How rude!

"Get your hands off me, woman!" came the shout of an angry voice from outside in the police stable yard.

Ella opened the door a crack to see what the commotion was about.

"Sheriff, you simply must help!" Marge the midwife beseeched, her arms wrapped about Axel's torso as he waved to the other guards to extract the small but determined woman who was not about to depart his presence of her own free will.

"I'm not falling for more of your cry wolf attempts to get me alone!" Axel snapped back at her. "You're a public menace!"

Ella's boot toe bumped the tack room door, and the movement caught Axel's eye. He hollered. "Who's there? Come out!"

Marge shrieked and darted behind Sheriff Axel, her hands clamped about his broad chest once more. "It's the murderer! I told you! You have to protect me!"

"And I told you to keep your hands to yourself!" Axel shouted, as the others came forward to his aid and peeled Marge off of their boss.

Ella stepped out from the tack room as another guard approached, and she shut the door behind her so as not to give Tom away.

"Why are you sneaking about here?" Axel demanded, slapping away Marge's groping hands.

"I was not sneaking," Ella replied haughtily, drawing herself up. She clutched the silver head of her stick and strode into the middle of the yard. "I'm...spot checking outbuildings. As duly elected council representative, for tax collection, and director of rents and repairs, I am well within my rights to er...." Ella patted her neckline for the chain of office but then recalled she'd loaned her official insignia to Willow, so stuck her nose in the air and avoided eye contact. "Conduct investigations into... ah, unauthorised veranda extensions."

"Whatever." Axel twitched as Marge's hand latched onto his thigh. Temper boiling over, he bellowed, "Get them both out of my sight!"

There was nothing to do but relent as the guards politely escorted Ella, and less-politely escorted the little midwife, out of the police yard gateway and into Northgate Square.

"Lady Ella! Thank mercy I found you! The sheriff won't listen to me!" Marge said the moment they were alone, her hands slapped in horror on her reddened cherub cheeks. "What you see before us has me scared witless." She pointed.

Across the wide square, a crowd had gathered on the town hall steps. Merlin stood with his publisher, Gwen. He in his roguish black leather jacket, and she in her eye-catching vivid red jacket. The couple were addressing Charmington townsfolk, mostly parents with their children. Cassidy and Bethany were also there. Little Bethany clutched onto the back of Cassidy's legs. Merlin held aloft what appeared to be one of his *Merlin's Magic For Beginners* textbooks to a smattering of applause.

Ella rolled her eyes. "Yes, it's frightening to behold. Merlin's shameless sales pitches. He doesn't even like children."

"I saw him attending the afternoon tea and then the mayor was killed!" Marge burbled on, ducking behind Ella. "I didn't know what to do!"

"I beg pardon?"

"The mystery man I saw yesterday morning! He's right there! Don't you see?"

Ella blinked as Marge's hysterical nonsense suddenly made sense. "You see *him*? The man Millie met with before she was crushed? Where?"

"There! There!" Marge shrieked, cowering behind Ella. She pointed into the crowd. "The handsome rogue!"

"Where? Is he standing *behind*...Merlin?"

Oh...bother.

"It is Merlin, isn't it?"

CHAPTER 22

THE ASTUTE

TOWN HALL STEPS, NORTHGATE SQUARE, CHARMINGTON.

Merlin was standing on the town hall steps with Gwen at his side, touting his new textbooks to a small gathering of parents as Ella approached across the square.

"My *Merlin's Magic for Beginners* is a complete and comprehensive set of detailed instructions that will bring out the latent ability in even the dullest student!" Merlin proclaimed boldly, holding aloft a sample book to show the curious parents. "Do we have a volunteer? I shall conduct a lesson."

The gathered crowd of citizens regarded each other and shuffled on the spot. Embarrassment and shyness overcoming the adults and their scattering of children. While the glimmer of success was a shiny lure, the ridicule of failure in front of neighbours and a notable figure was enough to douse the flame of ambition.

"Come along, there's no need to be shy!" Gwen chuckled, her laughter light and feminine. She pouted, flouncing her decorative array of pearls and golden chains. "Think of the fortunes that await your offspring. A career in magic can be very lucrative!"

Merlin caught sight of Ella moving towards him. "Why indeed, my own dear sister received a magic carpet as payment from the sultan of Constantinople!"

"It was a gift," Ella mumbled to herself. "Not technically a payment." Although, come to think of it, the sultan had given her the flying carpet after she had helped him out of a rather tricky situation. The gift was certainly an acknowledgement of a debt, if not exactly a payment.

"A magic carpet, people!" Merlin continued, trying to appeal to the crowd and win them over. "Worth more than *my* weight in gold."

Gwen patted his stomach. "And I think we can agree that is no small amount!" Her joke garnered a smattering of laughter, but still no volunteer.

His expression uncharacteristically earnest, Merlin looked at the many older faces in the crowd. "Does anyone here remember my sister, Cinderella? She used to stand in this very square when she was a small girl and robins and sparrows would come and sing to her. It was very pretty, was it not?"

There was a murmur of acknowledgement from the crowd. The older citizens within the gathering nodded at the nostalgic memory. Ella shut her eyes. Her mind cast back to her early days...

She, Sibylla, Merlin and Cinderella would scamper around this square, playing on the steps, while awaiting their parents to finish whatever affairs of state and tasks they had to make appearances for, or documents to sign, within the town hall. Cinderella would coax sparrows to come sit on her and Ella's hands while Sibylla and Merlin splashed in the unicorn water fountain, holding mock sea battles—much to the horror of their governess, as they froze the fountain waters and hurled icicles spears at each other with the recklessness of youth.

Ella sighed. How simple life had been back then.

"You there!" Merlin pointed into the crowd at Cassidy and Bethany. "Young lady, ask your little girl if she would like to coax a sparrow to land on her hand?"

Bethany's face uplifted, filled with a spark of joy and longing, but then she mumbled something about ruining her mittens and stepped back, her eyes downcast.

"Come along now, little girl," Merlin said eagerly, jogging down the steps to crouch down beside the pair. "Don't be obstinate. You won't get your mittens dirty."

"Wait!" said Cassidy, finding herself separated from Bethany as Gwen stepped between her and the child. "You don't understand!"

"It's a very simple task. Just hold your palm out like this..." Merlin grabbed Bethany's hand, removed the mitten, and held her palm up. "There, good, now I will tell you the magic words."

Bethany's eyes twinkled and in the stillness of held breaths she whispered, "I don't need words." She stretched her palm skyward.

The rays of daylight suddenly darkened as if a shadow had crossed the sun. Everyone looked up. A swirling black cloud rose beyond the town wall. And a cacophony of chirps lanced the air.

"Huh?" Gwen's brows furrowed. "What is that?"

"Magic preserve!" Ella elbowed through the people. "Birds!" Every bird in the forest judging from the noise. Oh, good gracious! Bethany's shyness was hiding more than a little wyld magical talent—the girl was an astute! A veritable force of nature.

Merlin blinked. Comprehension dawned, and his mouth split open to curse when Ella elbowed him aside.

The little girl giggled at the billowing roil of bird life displayed in the sky. Innocent sheer delight at the power of nature in her veins. Wyld magic at its rawest. Magic from the land itself.

Ella dropped her walking stick and grabbed Bethany by her hands. "Let's play a funny princess game!" Ella told the little girl. "Quick! Stand on my feet!"

Confused, but caught up in the moment of play—while around them every adult grabbed their nearest and dearest and ran and or flung themselves flat as the sky blackened and the gigantic swarm made up of every bird within the forest zoomed toward the unwitting herald that had called to them—Bethany stepped from the cobbles and balanced on the top of Ella's sturdy old boots.

"Don't fall off!" Ella laughed as they tottered about across the cobbles. "One, two, one, two!" Ella said, guiding the child's steps and spinning her around and around, trying to get Bethany to focus her attention on balancing and break focus on her unconscious desire to call the birds to her.

Sweet mercy, let this work! Ella begged silently. As her own magical power was under a binding spell, hopefully she would act as a dampener to the current of magic that had flowed between Bethany's raw wyld magic and the birds that must answer her call.

"It's a princess dance!" Ella cried. "This is how all princesses begin their dancing training."

"Are you really a princess?" Bethany giggled as they waltzed, while above them the gathering birds spiralled and swooped down. Closer and closer. Zeroing in on the child.

"I must be." Ella spun them, about, nearly out of breath. "The words 'Princess Ella' are stitched on my underwear."

The little girl burst into fits of laughter and above the square suddenly thousands of birds peeled away, abruptly released from the grip of the wyld magic power that had held them.

Breathlessly, Ella came to a complete stop and released Bethany's hold. Hands on thighs, Ella looked around at the cowering people who had sheltered wherever they could, their gaunt faces a mix of confusion but also fear. A lot of fear.

That needed to be dealt with swiftly. She looked about for Merlin, but he was leaning against a wall, bowed over, looking like he was going to throw up. No help there then. Typical.

"I'm so sorry, I should have been upfront with you," Cassidy said, hurrying forward and holding out Ella's stick for her, appearing pale-faced and with an expression that showed a mixture of regret and fear. "Betty suspected, but well…"

Before Cassidy could say anything else, Ella clasped her walking stick and waved off the young woman's unspoken fears. "No harm done. Unlike Sibylla, not a single goldfish boiled or duck scalded."

"Am I in trouble?" Bethany whispered, wide-eyed, as if realising she was the centre of the adult's attention.

"Not at all," Ella said, bending down to fix the small child with her warm gaze. She added, "You are a very clever child, and I think you are simply splendid! You remind me of my sister." She looked about the cobblestones and spied one of Merlin's textbooks that had been dropped and trampled on in the mad rush to take cover.

"Oh, my goodness," Ella intoned loudly, raising her voice to the trembling crowd, "to think this *ordinary* child exhibited astonishing magical ability after *one* lesson from the great Merlin! No doubt the child's future and *fortune* are assured!" She stooped to pick up the discarded textbook and flattened the bent cover. "I am going to tell all my friends to purchase a full set of *Merlin's Magic for Beginners* textbooks before this *extremely* limited supply sells out!"

"Oh, yes! I will too! I certainly intend to do so!" came the catch cry of gawking parents as the few display copies were suddenly prize objects. Coin purses unfastened with haste and jangled in front of Gwen, who was sourly dusting herself off, wiping snow and muddy leaves from her fashionable outfit.

"Gwen, my dear, allow me to offer you the use of my personal tax office so you may take orders and 'talk numbers', as they say." Ella gestured to Cassidy and locked gazes with Gwen. "Cassidy will show you the way, and then I expect you'll want to go discuss schooling options with Bethany's family, won't you, Gwen? How your publishing house will sponsor young Bethany with a full scholarship to Camelot Academy of Magic before another institution snaps her up, or claims her talent is inexplicably nothing to do with Merlin tutoring her today…"

Gwen's disgust at the mud on her outfit evaporated as Ella's hint struck at the woman in red's financial core. "I was about to say the same thing," Gwen said aloud to the crowd. "Indeed, Camelot Academic Press will offer several scholarships to *deserving* candidates' families who can testify that *Merlin's Magic for Beginners* is the ideal foundation for young minds..." She strutted off with Cassidy and Bethany, and a swathe of hopefully parents in her perfumed wake.

Wincing at the pain flaring in her knees because of her waltzing exertion, Ella hobbled over to where her brother remained, bowed over, hands on thighs, and whispering to himself, "Oh, sweet mercy! A raw astute!"

"Are you going to be sick?" Ella asked, lightly tapping his boot heel with the tip of her cane. "You've gone that colour after Sibylla dared you to eat your weight's worth in strawberries and cream."

Merlin jerked upright. Blood rushed back to his cheeks as he flicked his tousled hair into place. He spun around and cast her a scathing glare. "Smella, why ever didn't you tell me? A raw astute! That was a nasty trick! I could have had my flesh plucked from my bones and my eyes pecked out by those blasted sparrows!"

Ella rolled her eyes at her brother's melodramatics. "Hardly! And I didn't tell you because I didn't know." She shuffled off towards the police station where she'd left Tom testing the typewriters.

"That's jolly poor form!" Merlin growled, stomping after her. "You should be keeping an eye on this sort of thing, you know! Untrained astutes are very dangerous! Sibylla's ban doesn't mean wyld magic stops! It has to go somewhere!" Finished lecturing, he smoothed his shirt, and said, "Anyway, I admit you handled things well. I was going to step in, naturally, if you weren't up to the task. Um...and how did you get her to break concentration from the birds?"

Ella shrugged. "Magic pants."

"Fine, don't tell me," Merlin grumbled, turning away.

"Not so fast," Ella said, grabbing hold of him by his book satchel's strap. "Come with me. Tom and I need you to look over some typing samples. We might have found a clue to identify your blackmailer."

CHAPTER 23

THE TEST RESULTS

POLICE STATION, NORTHGATE SQUARE, CHARMINGTON.

On Ella's plea for discretion, Merlin and Ella crept into the police station courtyard, looking left and right as they snuck across the empty yard to the stable.

"What if it's been locked?" Merlin whispered, flattening himself against the stable wall outside the tack room.

"We might have both lost our magic temporarily, but nothing can take the Keys to the Kingdom gift from us," Ella said as the door lock gave way at her touch. She smiled smugly. "We are Charmings after all. While on Wyld soil, all locks give way to us."

"Ha! I forgot about that crummy so-called gift," Merlin uttered as they slipped into the tack room. Once more, the odorous polishing products assailed Ella's sense of smell. "Living in Avalon gave me a healthy respect for locks."

Ella arched an eyebrow at her brother. "Let me guess. You got cornered by angry husbands while chasing after married women?"

"No, I mean I literally banged my face into doors which unexpectedly didn't open! A lifetime of doors opening at my touch was a hard habit to break!" He scowled at the thought and rubbed his nose. "Our ancestors must have been robber barons or some such to value such a stupid power. Anyway, I see the typewriters, but where is your talkative cat?"

"You can come out," Ella said, peering underneath the large worktable on which the typewriters were laid out. "It's just me."

But Tomcat's furry white form did not emerge from a hiding place.

"That's odd..." Ella straightened. Tom was gone, but the paper he had been using as a typing sample to test the machines was still there, fed into the last in the line-up, the small portable model typewriter labelled 'Hyde'.

"Aha! What a brilliant test!" Merlin extolled, extracting his magnifying glass from the book satchel. "If the culprit's machine is among one of these, I will be able... Oh! Yes! This is definitely the one my blackmailer used...but..." He stood back as if startled. Then leaned in for another look.

"What's wrong?" Ella said, having opened a few cupboards to double check Tom wasn't hiding within. "You observed the minute difference in the letter S so quickly? Do the lines look normal?"

"Come see for yourself," Merlin said, standing back and gesturing to the sheet within the small portable model. "The lines look normal, well as normal as a row of inexplicable *bosoms* can look until it dissolves into dark rambling thoughts..."

Ella read:

```
Bosom. BoSom. SsS. BOSOM. Bosom.  Why? Bosom.
Why not give up? Bosom.  No one cares for
Bosom. Cares for you.  This is pointleSS. YOU
are pointleSS.  Pointless. Stupid. WorthleSs.
```

Ella was shocked. "Magic preserve! What happened here? This is quite out of character for Tom—he's always so positive."

Merlin returned the magnifying glass to the satchel. "*Magic* being the operative word." He shuffled Ella aside and rolled up his sleeves. "Out of the way, Smella. This calls for an expert."

Ella sighed at his theatrics, but stood back. Merlin squatted down so his head was level with the typewriters. Then he shut his eyes. A moment later, his grey eyes snapped open. "Aha! Don't you smell it?" He leaned forward and sniffed the keys. "That distinct hint of corruption?"

Ella gestured to bottles, polishing cloths, squares of beeswax, and other paraphernalia used to keep the saddles and leather harness in top condition. "All I can smell are the bottles of Iron Drake shoe polish."

Merlin tipped the small typewriter back and forth and then peered at the keys and underneath the carriage. "If typing ribbons laced with black magic had been used, even many years ago, the keys could have built up a coating of evil not perceivable to the human eye."

"A cursed typewriter..." Ella pursed her lips. "Hmm, and young Tom is exceptionally sensitive to black magic. Even a trace of it made him very ill the first time we first met Prince John. A cursed typewriter would certainly explain this sudden spewing of dark rambling thoughts." She regarded the type-test again with dismay.

"This certainly helps explain my lunatic blackmailer's behaviour!" Merlin looked over his shoulder at her. "Over time, the compounded use of a cursed typewriter would corrupt or poison the original user's mind, regardless of their initial sensitivity."

"Save your lectures for beginners," Ella responded primly. "Black magic's influencing effect is one-oh-one. Might I remind you, I graduated top of my class."

"Maybe don't continue to tell people that," Merlin jibed as he wiped his fingers on a polishing rag. "Coming top of black magic isn't quite the accolade you think it is."

Ella paced the small room, talking aloud as she thought. "Cursed objects often develop personalities... If we assume this typewriter held dominant influence over its owner—it could even have *planned* Millie's demise." Ella nodded. "Very well. I agree with your theory."

Merlin tapped the cardboard labelled 'Hyde', tied to the small typewriter. "And you'll then concede to my theory that Doctor Edison Hyde, as the owner of the cursed contraption, is also my blackmailer?" Merlin's eyes glowed triumphantly. "It's typical of the man. He has no imagination. Exactly the simple-minded dumpling to be swayed by murderous murmurings from these evil-coated keys."

"Tosh! You cannot be serious as to suggest that an intelligent man of logic and science like Doctor Hyde is in the thrall of an evil typewriter?" Ella folded her arms. "The notion is ridiculous. He—or any doctor, for that matter—would have recognised the symptoms and treated himself for the side-effects of black magic."

Noise from out in the police yard just then drew their attention. Merlin's eyes bulged. Doctor Hyde was on the back step of the police station, talking with Axel.

"Let's ask him!" Merlin blurted, heading out the tack room door before Ella could stop him. "Come to turn yourself in?" Merlin shouted at Hyde as he strode out into the wintery daylight, with Ella in his wake. "That's jolly good of you!"

"In a manner of speaking," Hyde explained, his expression fraught with anguish. He nodded acknowledgement to Ella. "As I told Lady Ella when the mayor died of apparent poisoning, it immediately occurred that my poisons safe could have been tampered with—And the theft of my office typewriter merely a diversion. So I weighed and measured everything." Hyde shuffled on the step. "Ahem. I regret to report a lethal dose of arsenic was missing."

"Arsenic," Axel murmured, crossing his arms and leaning against the doorframe. "Are you confessing to the mayor's murder? Criminals aren't usually so helpful."

"Why do you even have a stash of poisons?" Merlin added, jabbing an accusing finger. "That's extremely suspicious."

"I'm not confessing," Hyde snapped, nerves clearly fraying at Axel's glib attitude and Merlin's needling. "And I don't *stash them*—I remove poisons whenever I find them. I keep them in my safe only until they can be disposed of properly! I'm coming forward, Sheriff, so you can rule me out of the investigation—"

"A cunning plan!" Merlin interjected snidely to Ella, who rolled her eyes.

"Furthermore! The mayor's death needs to be investigated," Hyde added emphatically. "Arsenic remains a hypothesis *only* until conclusive evidence is found to confirm the cause of death." Doctor Hyde turned, pleaded his case to the sheriff. "I offered the family my services in performing an autopsy, but they declined."

"Hardly surprising," Merlin sneered at the doctor's back. "All that pulling brains out noses and stuffing kidneys in pots."

Hyde spun around. "That's mummification, you *insufferable* oaf!"

"Whatever. No one wants your new age, hippy dippy autopsy—we use magic around here!" Merlin broke off, as if sharply reminded that he'd lost his powers for the time being. "Anyway. Not the point. Sheriff, arrest this man. He's a blackmailer!"

"What?" Doctor Hyde flinched. Looking utterly aghast, he cast a confused glance at Ella and the sheriff.

"Don't deny it, Edison. We have your labelled typewriter as proof!" Merlin pushed past Ella and quickly fetched the small typewriter from the tack room and handed it to the doctor.

Doctor Hyde squinted at the dangling square of cardboard with his name on it. "Of course I deny such a charge! That *isn't* my typewriter. Even if you have recovered some stolen ones, *anyone* could have swapped the labels—or mislabelled them." He looked over his shoulder at Axel, who held his hands up in a gesture of *nothing-to-do-with-me*.

"They were labelled like that when they brought them in from the collapsed display." Axel snatched the typewriter from Merlin's hands and chucked the little typewriter into the tack room, where it bounced with an oddly wounded mechanical chime upon the worktable. "This is an ongoing investigation—which I might add, you're interfering with. That is a crime." The sheriff slammed the door shut and locked it again. Placing the key in his pocket, he rattled the doorhandle to make sure it had locked. "Whatever dispute you two *gentlemen* have, take it far away. I do not care." Axel's eye caught Ella's. "And if I find you sneaking around my yard again, unauthorised verandas be damned, I will lock you up too!"

"I say!" Hyde turned from arguing with Merlin to jump to Ella's defence. "That's uncalled for!"

Unrepentant, Axel waved them off. "Everyone get out. I have dozens of tedious amnesty items to catalogue before I can go home tonight and the next upper class prat that annoys me today is getting my boot up their—"

"We apologise for the interruption," Ella interjected, tugging her brother's sleeve. "Thank you for your service."

"You, Doctor, you're with me. We'll finish your report of stolen arsenic inside," Axel uttered, not looking back. And Doctor Hyde, with a quick bow to Ella, followed the sheriff into the back of the police station.

"We can't just leave it!" Merlin grumbled as Ella shunted him, still protesting, out the gate into Northgate Square. "He's right there! The typewriter is proof Hyde's my blackmailer! Label switching be damned!"

Ella pointed to the row of buildings across the square. "Come. We'll go to the haberdashery. Hopefully Sally will remember which was whose and be able to confirm if Hyde is speaking the truth."

"Good plan, sis." Merlin nodded. Placated, he tugged up the lapels of his leather jacket. "Once Sally confirms Hyde is the true owner of that cursed typewriter, then he can't deny he's my blackmailer—and I can get my manuscript back! Nothing can stop us now!"

CHAPTER 24

TOM CRIES FOUL
WHILE MERLIN BEWITCHES

NORTHGATE SQUARE, CHARMINGTON.

"Good mother Ella! Wait!" called a voice, accompanied by a peculiar jangling like wind chimes.

Willow jogged into view from between two buildings. "Everyone is looking for you! I sent Cheapcuts to the castle in case you were there." Out of breath, the young witch leaned over, hands on thighs of her bright patchwork coat. "You must come at once." She pointed back the way she came. "It's Tom! There's something dreadfully wrong. He's very upset. I don't know what's going on."

"Cursed," Merlin mouthed with a jaunty tilt of his head. "What did I tell you?" He huffed across his knuckles and polished them on his jacket front. His smug expression faltered when Ella changed directions and joined Willow. "No, Ella! The haberdashery is right there! Oh, you can't be serious. He's just a cat!"

"He is not *just* a cat!" Ella snapped. "He's *my* cat! You go talk to Sally—actually on second thoughts. You stay with me!" Ella back tracked and grabbed Merlin by his bag strap. She towed him reluctantly after her and Willow. "Come along, I won't have you upsetting Sally even more than she already is! If Tom is suffering the effects of a black magic curse, then, as our self-titled magic expert, you had better come with me and fix it!"

"WHAT DO YOU MEAN, TOM is stuck in a chimney?" Ella asked as she traipsed after Willow down Baker Street toward the Fairweather orphanage.

"He's not stuck—or at least I don't think so! He just won't come down," Willow explained, clearly distressed. She removed the golden chain of office and handed it back to Ella as they hurried. "We were using the fireplace as a safe place to test for elemental powers, you know, having the children try to start a fire using magic when Tom rushed in." Willow opened a side door for Ella and ushered her and Merlin through the warren of rooms to a front parlour where there was a bit of a disturbance going on.

Mistress Fairweather was standing, hands on hips, towering over the three orphans. Sandy and Sam, in their humble blue and yellow knitted sweaters and Olly, dressed in ill-fitting black silk. Fairweather was giving them a right telling off. "Which of you bewitched it? I turn my back for five minutes and the chimney is talking! This is a respectable orphanage!" Mistress Fairweather boomed. "We don't stand for the likes of talking chimneys!"

The matron started on seeing Ella behind her.

"My deepest apologies," Ella tried to placate. Quite aware that she needed to get the matron back on her side if Ella was going to be of any use as a character reference for Sally's adoption of young Olly. "As Charmington's director of rents and repairs, I take full responsibility."

The matron crossed her muscular arms across her broad bosom. "Talking chimneys may be all the rage in *decadent* foreign places, but I won't have it, I tell you!"

"I quite agree with you, madam," Merlin intoned pleasantly, making himself known. "Forgive me, my dear lady, introductions have not been made. I am Merlin Charming. At your service..." And he bowed formally, like a gallant knight presented to his queen.

"Ohh..." Mistress Fairweather looked Merlin up and down. Her brusque air dissolved. She wet her lips, blushed and clutched her shawl to her chest. "I know who you are...sir." She bobbed a wobbly curtsy.

"My dear lady, would it be too *forward* of me to request a..." He looked deep into the matron's eyes and held her gaze "...a *private* tour of this fine establishment?" Merlin offered her his arm. "I have been told this orphanage is the epitome of modern economy and efficiency."

Ella barely refrained from pulling a sour face as the enraptured matron glided arm in arm with Merlin out into the narrow hallway, her voice taking on a light shy, feminine lilt as Merlin asked her inane questions of the building's history.

Whatever the ladies saw in her brother, she would never know!

"Tom!" Willow called, awkwardly leaning over the brass fireguard and speaking into the fireplace. "Ella is here! Won't you come down now?"

"Please come down!" Sandy, Sam and Olly added.

A pinch of soot dislodged from the chimney. "Go away!" came a muffled sob.

"Let's move this..." Ella instructed the children, and Sandy and Willow shifted the brass fireguard out of the way. Ella braced herself with her stick and crouched on the plain rag rug.

"Tom, are you all right?" Ella called up the chimney breast. "I was anxious when you disappeared."

"No, you weren't," Tomcat's mournful voice retorted from the chimney breast and more soot rained down. "You don't care. No one cares. Why should they?"

Ella blanched as soot pinged down on the grate. "Oh dear, he's climbing further up!"

"I'll get him!" Olly cried. The little child pushed past Ella before she could stop them. They ducked under the lintel.

Ella and Willow both shrieked, grabbing at Olly's legs disappearing up the chimney. The child wriggled and came suddenly free. Ella tumbled back. A cloud of soot puffed into the parlour. Olly blinked, face black as their mourning frock, but they grinned triumphantly at the filthy, soot-coated cat in their arms.

Sandy and Sam thumped Olly on the shoulders while Willow helped Ella to her feet with the aid of her walking stick.

Ella winced at the soot now coating the hearthrug, the scent of coal tar heavy on the room. This mess would not please Mistress Fairweather.

With the timing of all great tragic plays, the matron and Merlin re-entered the room.

Fairweather's look of adoration cracked like a shattered window and she drew a deep breath when Merlin suddenly thrust himself into the flame of her kindled wrath. "My cat! You found my beloved cat!" Merlin swept Tomcat into his arms. Tomcat began bawling tears, and Merlin hugged Tomcat to his chest, wrapping his leather coat across the filthy creature as Mistress Feather stood staring at the mess, her mouth agape.

"Darling child, you have saved my most cherished kitty cat!" Merlin patted Olly on the head and beamed at Fairweather. "My dear lady, these noble, kind-hearted children are a credit to your fine upbringing. I insist on rewarding them with cakes and cordial. We shall go now. Immediately. Follow me children!"

"But..." Mistress Fairweather began, dismay etched on her face.

Merlin touched his finger to the matron's lips. "I have not forgotten. I will send my carriage for you...tonight."

Ella and Willow quickly ushered the children out of the parlour, leaving the matron standing dazed, a smudge of soot on her lips.

"I promise I shall behave as a gentleman tonight..." Merlin kissed the air and, closing the door, added with a wink, "Unless you say otherwise!"

CHAPTER 25

MAGIC TOUCH DAY SPA

MAGIC TOUCH DAY SPA, EAST AVENUE, UPPER EAST CHARMINGTON.

"I'll do the talking," Ella said as the rather forlorn and sooty group huddled behind her on the steps and she rang the doorbell of the stylish, upper-east side establishment.

A moment later, the door swung open and the enthusiastic greeting, "Welcome to Magic Touch Day Spa..." tumbled from Goldilocks lips before dying.

The little lady with the immaculate pink bouffant hairdo blinked up at Ella's apologetic smile, and beheld three adults, three children—one who had a rat peeking out her jumper neckline—and a wailing cat. All in various states of sootiness, from slight to extreme.

Goldi tapped her patent leather pumps on the white stone threshold of her business. "I can see what needs to be done, Ella, but I don't believe there's anything you can say to convince me to let your grimy lot in."

"Free rent for a month?"

Goldi's lips pushed out. "That'll do. Not the front door!" She held up a tiny hand to stop the collective from entering. "Round back! I'll not have soot tramped into my Persian carpets!"

ELLA, MERLIN, WILLOW AND THE orphans soon found themselves experiencing the luxuries of Goldi's day spa first hand. The adults were all swiftly cleansed and refreshed. One of Goldi's assistants even gave Mr. Rat a gentle bath in a hand nail basin, followed by a groom and a nail clip.

Then, once the adults sat wrapped in soft white fluffy robes, lounging in plush leather chairs, it was the orphan's turn for a cleanse and makeover. They complained loudly at having to endure their hair being washed and combed by Goldi's army of capable assistants, but they enjoyed the offerings of fresh fruit. Melon slices, grapes, and the like were expensive luxuries that were not about to be turned down. Even more enthusiastically, Sam, Sandy and Olly applied floral scented creams and lotions to their hands, and drew moustaches on each other's faces with any unattended pot of floral scented lotion.

While this was going on, Goldi herself, masked and gloved, took charge of Tom's treatment. She instructed an assistant to place the weeping Tomcat in a large steaming basin filled with bubble bath, various herbs and rose petals, and then began the thorough job of removing all traces of soot and black magic residue from his fur. Willow, hair wrapped in a white towel to match her white bathrobe, peered intently at the process and asked Goldi lots of questions about the ratio of herbal tinctures added to the water to aid the cleansing process.

Seemingly disinterested, as if the whole affair was an everyday occurrence, Merlin ignored everything and sat back, bored, with slices of cucumbers on his eyelids and a freshly made strawberry cocktail clutched in his hand.

While it had been many years since Ella had enjoyed the pampering of a high-class day spa, as she sat back, a towel across her shoulders and her freshly combed damp curls dripping with rose petal scented water, she could not relax, but drummed her fingernails on the leather armchair and thought over the past two days' events. This task was less easy to concentrate on as Tom kept bursting into tears and the orphans were noisily challenging each other to catch grapes in their mouths which they tossed from across the room.

A grape suddenly plopped into Tom's basin, where Goldi worked, and Willow observed. The orphan's cast guilty glances as Tomcat blinked at the grape and burst out in another slew of tears, proclaiming loudly, "Nobody wants bathwater grape! It's like me! I'm the grape!" He swiped a sodden paw across his cat face. "That's why my parents gave me away! That's why Cassidy wants to leave town!"

All at once, the orphans huddled around his basin, soothing and hushing his fears. "Family is who ya make it," Olly said. "We're your family now."

"Yeah!" Sandy and Sam cheered loyally. "Baker Street orphans forever!"

Goldi rolled back out of the way of the orphan group on her little roller chair. "Tom's treatment is going to require a change of water," Goldi muttered to Willow, waving one of her workers over as the orphans formed a big giant hug around Tom.

Tugging her mask down, Goldi ventured over to Ella. "I'll just oversee the girls throwing out the curse-tainted residue. It must be disposed of properly, and then I'll have your knee pain sorted in no time."

Ella nodded, and while the orphans continued consoling Tom, saying how much they loved him and all the wonderful things he'd done—mentioning several adventures they had had together that were entirely unbeknownst to Ella—she leaned back into the soft leather chair. "Throw out...? Disposed of properly? Hmm..."

"What are you thinking?" Merlin asked, lifting a cucumber slice from his eyelid to peer at her.

"You recall what Tom discovered. About the extra typewriter? And we wondered if someone could have dropped the typewriter from above the writers' walk display?"

Merlin nodded. "Yes, yes, to create a chain reaction."

Ella lifted her chin to where Tom was being lifted from the bath and bundled into a towel. "What if the person was no longer in the thrall of the cursed typewriter but was aware of its evil influence? What if, given the chance, they had simply been trying to *throw* it away?"

Merlin grimaced. "Hardly an orthodox approach, throwing a typewriter out an office window! But...given if they were suffering delusions, they may have rather a shaky grip on what was a sensible plan. Curses do affect people differently."

"Agreed. So we can't rule it out. Rather than being a deliberate act to cause harm, they could have simply been desperately trying to rid themselves of the cursed typewriter."

"Ha!" Merlin sat back and placed the cucumber slices over his eyes once more. "We can rule it out because it *was* Hyde's typewriter. Does he have regular access to the rooms and offices above the walkway? I think not. Which means he was there by design, by *deliberate* intent. I was standing under that walkway seconds before... before..." Merlin shuddered. "I don't want to think about it any more." He swirled the ice around in his glass and then sipped his strawberry cocktail noisily through his straw.

"Hyde claimed it wasn't his typewriter, and I believed him. After all, what is his motive?"

"Motive?" Merlin sneered. "First, black magic curses don't need motives—they just influence people's fears and desires—which you're forgetting is completely in line with Hyde. The chap is horrendously jealous of my success."

"Maybe he—or whoever—was trying to fight against the evil influence? Their method may have been ill-advised, but perhaps their intentions were true even if their actions were desperate?"

"Ill-advised? Do you even hear yourself? My beautiful Millie was crushed! Crushed right before my eyes. I see it every time I close them!" He wrenched the cucumber off his eyes. "What happened to you, sis? When did you ever look for people's better intentions? It's like I don't know you any more—if I weren't so foolish, I might say that you, too, were under the influence of something or someone."

"I am." Ella nodded to Tomcat's curled form, wrapped in a big bath towel as Goldi's assistants refilled his bubble bath. "Someone better than me. Someone who tries to see the best in everyone." She swept the towel off her hair. "I am going to investigate the offices above the walkway for clues. Are you coming or staying?"

"Ugh!" Merlin growled, gulping down the rest of the fruity drink. "Fine! But only to prove that I am right! That whoever threw that typewriter out the window did so to hide their blackmail attempts. *Hyde* being the word of the day!"

CHAPTER 26

MARLEY'S OFFICE AND THE MESSENGER

OFFICES WITHIN THE TOWN HALL, Northgate Square, Charmington.

"This jolly well has to be it," Merlin muttered doggedly, a phrase he had used several times in the last half hour as he and Ella trudged along the hallways of the various offices that overlooked the stone archway.

Ella held her tongue and glanced at the brass nameplate which read: *J Marley. Accountant.* So far, they had barged into the offices of three accountants, two lawyers and a philatelist.

Merlin yanked the door open and charged through, shouting jovially, "Spot inspection! Hide your whiskey! Ha ha!" He drew up short and cast a glance over his shoulder at Ella. "No one here..."

"Indeed," Ella came to the same conclusion as they entered the cramped but luxurious small office stuffed with book-lined shelves and a paper strewn, heavy dark oak desk next to a large sash window.

She followed Merlin to the window, and he lifted the sash to a blast of wintery air, setting all the paperwork on the desk fluttering. "Aha!" Merlin leaned out, then in again. "We have a winner! Dead centre above the walkway! This has to be our spot! I bet my reputation Hyde launched the typewriter from here."

Ella glanced out the window and down at the archway three flights below. "It appears so. I concede the location—but I won't let you besmirch Doctor's Hyde's name. There's still no proof he was involved." She drew her cloak tight as the wind swirled. They were quite high up, but even with the gusting winds, if someone had dropped the typewriter from this height, its weight would have ensured it held its course as it plummeted... Ella shuddered.

Seemingly unperturbed by the icy blast or the height, Merlin rested his elbows on the sill. "What a view! You can see everything from here. Look, there's the haberdashery!" He pointed, and a crestfallen expression suddenly crossed his features. "I understand young Tom's pain, you know... You think I'm all bluster and vinegar, but I feel it too. The pain of rejection."

"Rejection?" Ella arched an eyebrow. What was this? Had something happened to Tom that he hadn't told her?

Merlin nodded. "I felt horrible—utterly devastated—when Sally gave me the bad news all those years ago." He rubbed his left hand ring finger as if imagining a wedding ring. "How different my life would be if I had married Millie."

"What are you referring to?" Ella felt a sting of regret mixed with confusion. "Has young Tom confided in you?" Ella thought back to what Tom had spoken of earlier, that Cassidy was thinking of moving to Nottingham. Was there more to it than she realised?

Merlin gripped the windowsill. "Gwen! Where is she going at this hour?" He freed his pocket watch from his inside jacket pocket and flicked the gold cover open to reveal the time. "She should be at Claude's, setting up for the book signing at six." He shook his head and tucked the watch away. "Speaking of, I better make a move, so I'm not late myself. Those leather bound special commemorative editions of my *Guide* won't sign themselves!"

Ella stood clear from the window frame so her brother could slide the sash closed. "But I thought you said a *late* entrance makes a *great* entrance?"

"Yeah, but you have to know your audience, sis." Merlin patted her shoulder. "And Claude was an actor. Actors *live* for impeccable timing."

Just then, someone slid a note under the door of the office.

A note addressed to Merlin.

"What the deuce!" Merlin blurted. He reached for the folded square, but Ella stepped around him and yanked the door open.

"Marge!" Ella cried, coming face to face with the little blonde midwife, who blanched and shrieked, before legging off down the corridor.

"What's it say?" Ella enquired of her brother.

Merlin unfolded the paper. A handwritten message. He cleared his throat. "We must meet in person. You need to know the truth. I will be at Claude's at half-past six precisely."

Ella gripped the silver head of her cane. "You get to your six o'clock book signing. I will deal with Marge and catch up with you at Claude's."

Merlin nodded and Ella limped after the midwife's fading footsteps echoing along the hallway. Magic preserve. What is the world was Marge up to?

MARGE HAD A HEAD START and a fair turn of speed, but Ella had just spent the past forty minutes traipsing these hallways and offices and knew every turn. The midwife's little boots tapped a rhythm down the wooden staircase, heralding her exact path. And though Ella had a limp, there was nothing wrong with her hearing, and on recognising the *whump-whump* of a landing door, Ella knew she had the little midwife cornered...

Ella pushed open the door to the landing of the portrait gallery where row upon row of mayoral portraits hung on the walls of the corridor preceding the mayoral office. At the far end of the gallery, Marge threw a smirk over her shoulder at Ella and then gripped the chamber door handle.

Locked. A dead end. On realising her mistake, Marge spun around and pressed her back to the solid oak door as Ella limped closer, her cane tapping hollowly against the floorboards.

Consternation flooded the midwife's usually bubbly features. Her dimples faltered as she held up her hand. "Wait! Lady Ella. It's not what it seems."

Ella gripped her walking stick. She regarded the midwife. Twice this day, Marge had tried to convince Ella that Merlin—or at least, a mysterious stranger—was mixed up in Millie's tragic demise. Was Marge's involvement truly a coincidence or by design? Was Marge hiding something? "So you *didn't* write that note to my brother?"

Marge blinked. "Brother? I didn't know Merlin was your brother." The little midwife shook her blonde curls. "What I mean is, I'm just the messenger. I didn't write that note—well, *technically* I wrote it—but that's because they paid me to pass on the message in person. But well..." Marge clutched at the hem of her red cape. "I didn't want to put myself in danger! You know how it is. Powerful men like Merlin always get away with their crimes!"

"Crimes? What crimes?" Ella sighed. "Whereas *you* were motivated by greed, but chickened out. So instead you wrote the note and slid it under the door. That's how it seems to me. Have I missed anything?"

"It's got nothing to do with me. I swear." Without meeting her eye, Marge said cagily, "I *could* tell you on whose behalf I was acting. But that would be two small favours you owed me... Or perhaps one big favour?"

Ella drew a sharp, angry breath. Magic preserve! And to think for a moment that morning she had thought Marge might be on the verge of learning the error of her ways! How foolish she had been to think so. If anyone had been taught a lesson, it was Ella. Marge had evolved from wanton gossip mongering to extortion!

"*Who* told you to deliver the message?" Ella demanded, banging her cane tip hard against the oak floorboards.

Marge gulped, "It was Tobias."

CHAPTER 27

ALL THE WORLD'S A STAGE

TOWN HALL ALLEYWAY, NORTHGATE SQUARE, CHARMINGTON.

"Tobias?" Ella mumbled to herself as she shuffled across the frosty cobbles in the lee of the town hall. She turned the idea around and around in her mind. Whatever could Tobias have to tell Merlin? Could Tobias know who Merlin's blackmailer was? Could Tobias be the blackmailer? But if so, what did he have to gain? All Tobias ever seemed to desire was for someone to publish one of his romance novels and, seemingly, that was going to happen shortly... Sally had told her as much the day before.

Well, undoubtedly the answer lay in getting to the book signing at Claude's.

Only time now would reveal what Tobias was planning on doing, or telling Merlin, at half-past six. But surely it must be telling—the schoolmaster must have information to pass along. If someone was actually planning on hurting Merlin, surely they wouldn't be able to do anything at the book signing when surrounded by so many people? Then again, someone had poisoned the mayor in similar circumstances!

Mulling this dreadful thought over, Ella spotted a person in an emerald cloak leaning against a stone wall nearby the archway walkway, which was still being guarded by the two castle guards she had commanded to cordon off the area earlier that day. The older man and the young woman in the ill-fitting uniform were marching back and forth, pikes held aloft as they patrolled the alley.

Emerald cloak? Was that the same horrid man who had shouted at Gwen?

Possibly, though, she couldn't see their face, obscured as it was by the green hood. She better have a word with them! But her cane tapping against the ground as she approached alerted the emerald cloaked person to turn her way. They started. Pivoted on their heels as if to run.

Not again! What was it with people running away today?

"Guards! Stop that man!" Ella commanded the two castle guards, clutching their pikes.

Which they did.

Much to the surprise of the cloaked figure, who squirmed in their grasp. "Unhand me! What are you playing at?" the emerald cloak person cried. Their struggles pushed back the hood to reveal a pasty complexion and thinning ginger hair.

"Tobias!" Now it was Ella's turn to be surprised. Could it really have been the mild-mannered teacher that she overheard berating Gwen? "Were you wearing this cloak earlier?"

"Huh?" Tobias blinked. Panicked or confused, he kept attempting to shrug off the grip of the pair of castle guards, but they held firm. "Claude gave it to me when he bought a new cloak this afternoon."

"What are you doing lurking around here?" Ella probed the schoolmaster, gesturing to the stone archway and the forlorn remnants of the writers' walk display.

"Answer her!" snapped the younger guard, as her older companion pulled all manner of menacing faces, glaring, leering and growling at their captive.

"What are you playing at?" Tobias grumbled at the leering pair holding him. And then to Ella, "I was waiting here for Spalding—but the fellow is a no show. I must hurry. I urgently need to be at Claude's. If I don't leave now, I will miss the book signing."

"What is the urgency?" Ella narrowed her eyes. "So much fuss over getting your first edition *Guide* book signed?"

"I can't explain," Tobias implored. "You must let me go. Time is of the essence!"

"We'll be the judge!" the old guard growled, his bared teeth next to Tobias' ear. "Or you'll be spending your time at 'er Majesty's leisure!"

The female guard nudged her comrade in the ribs and whispered, "Oh! Good improv, Bob."

Ella frowned. Were the guards, perhaps, taking their role a little too far? She dismissed the notion and instead decided not to waste their enthusiasm. "Since Tobias won't answer my questions. Guards, take him to the castle dungeon for further questioning."

"Aye! Aye!" the older one cried as the younger saluted with the wrong hand.

Tobias' mouth dropped open. "Guards? These aren't guards," he blurted, stunned and appalled. "Tell her you're not a guard, Bob!"

Bob frowned and released Tobias. "I say, Toby, old chap, you made me break character! Super bad form!" He grumbled to his younger companion, who likewise tutted at Tobias, adding, "You're supposed to call '*scene*'!"

Ella blinked. "Someone better tell me what is going on here."

Exasperated, Tobias threw his hands up in the air. "This is Bob and Fishstix! They're Pickford Players. Actors in the same company as Spalding."

"Encountering your Ladyship this afternoon was impeccable timing," Bob replied, picking up his dropped pike. He also seemed to have dropped his thick rural accent as he explained, "We were researching spear carrier roles via the fashionable 'method acting' for Nigella's Christmas play."

The young woman nodded. "We don't know what play it's gonna be, but there are always parts for spear carriers. Well-known fact."

Ella rolled her eyes. Magic preserve! Writers and actors! They were a peculiar bunch. Even while brushing off this development, she couldn't resist adding a, "Your name is *Fish Sticks*?"

The young woman shrugged. "It's a long story." She unbuckled the over-sized helm, removed it, wiped her brow and then bowed. "We must be on our way. It was a pleasure working with you. Your Highness." Fishstix and Bob slung their pikes over their shoulders, calling to the schoolmaster as they departed, "See you later!"

"Anyway," Ella said to Tobias, moving on with the larger matter at hand before he took it in his mind to run off again. "If you truly have nothing to hide, you won't mind explaining the real reason you are so desperate to meet my brother in person."

Tobias scrubbed his hands to his face and then sighed. "Very well." He stared at his boots a moment as if to gather his thoughts and then said, "I guess it began about two months ago. When Millie discovered Sally's dark secret."

"Sally has a dark secret?" Ella baulked, pulling her cloak tight about her.

"Quite so," the schoolmaster said, nodding grimly. Mimicking her gesture, he wrapped his own emerald-green cloak close. "Uncovering the secret set off the sister's recent feuding."

"And? What is the secret?"

"Sally told Merlin a lie fifty years ago. A lie about Millie..."

CHAPTER 28

THE SECRET BEHIND THE FEUD REVEALED

TOWN HALL ALLEYWAY, NORTHGATE SQUARE, CHARMINGTON.

"A lie?" Ella leaned heavily on her walking stick. While the twilight of approaching sunset had drained the last of the warmth from the watery daylight and set Ella's bones shivering, even the thought of a hot chocolate beside a large welcoming fireside would not draw her from this shadowy spot. Not until she learned the truth behind the haberdashery sister's feud. "Sally told Merlin a lie about Millie? A lie about her own dear sister?"

Tobias paced about on the spot, as if not sure where to begin, or perhaps, like Ella, feeling the cold seep into his bones as the shadows cast by the archway loomed over them. "Yes... About two months ago, Merlin sent Millie a letter. He wanted her help with local research for a book or something. I'm not sure about the details of the book. But anyway, in this letter, he apparently mentioned something about regrets and water under the bridge. That kind of thing. Merlin wrote he was completely at peace now, and acknowledged that things had worked out for them both when they broke off their relationship."

Ella nodded. "I'm with you so far. Indeed, common knowledge around here. Merlin broke Millie's heart." Ella shook her head. To think she had such a thoughtless brother. He really was the worst!

"Ah! But here's the thing." Tobias held up a finger and lowered his voice. "In the letter, Merlin mentioned Millie *changing her mind* and turning down his marriage proposal."

"She what?" Ella blanched at this. Surely it was the other way around! Or at least, that Merlin had never proposed when Millie was expecting him to? "Go on, I'm listening."

"It was then that Millie realised Sally had lied to Merlin." Tobias glanced over his shoulder, as if afraid of being overheard. "You see, Millie told *me she* accepted Merlin's proposal!"

Ella gasped. A memory flitted into her mind—only a few hours ago Merlin had been blathering on about all the women he had proposed to! Barely a baker's dozen, he said! Magic preserve, so he *had* asked

Millie to marry him! "But if Millie *had* accepted the proposal, then how on earth did he think she had changed her mind?"

Tobias frowned. "That's the twist. You see, Sally was the one in the middle delivering their messages." Tobias placed hands on hips and tutted. "And so Millie deduced that Sally must have told Merlin that Millie changed her mind, cold feet or whatever. And that's why Merlin left town. Not because, as Sally told Millie, Merlin was living up to his heart-breaker reputation, and chasing after a fabulous opportunity in Avalon to make his mark."

"Sally *lied* to Millie?" Ella mulled this revelation over. "Why would she do that?" Although an appalling concept, there was a grain of truth. "Uncovering a lie of such magnitude would definitely explain the cause of the sister's feud."

Tobias nodded sadly. "Yes." He turned around on the spot. "Indeed, I'm sure you've noticed. Things have not been well between the pair for many weeks..."

"How did you become involved?"

Tobias sighed. Pulling his cloak close again, he paced back and forth across the cobbles as if to ward off the chill or ease his troubled mind. "At first, Millie was going to write to Merlin, to explain the truth." He paused and smiled at the memory. "She turned to me to help draft the letter. I guess as a writer of the heart, she thought I could help mend old fences." He puffed up his chest, as if proud to be asked to do the task, but then all pride evaporated as he physically sagged and added forlornly, "But then Sally talked Millie out of it. Said, knowing the truth would only open up old wounds. Make things worse for Merlin."

"Especially as Merlin is with Gwen now..."

"Yes, I see that now... but..." Tobias dragged a hand through his thinning hair. "But the injustice of Sally's actions stirred me to anger." He curled a fist, his pale complexion wracked with anguish. "I...I felt I had to *do* something! Anything! So last month, I wrote to Merlin's publisher and told her the truth myself..."

Ella was aghast. "You wrote and told Gwen! Told Gwen that Merlin's former true love had accepted his proposal!" Magic preserve! What consequences might Tobias' meddling have put into play? Imagine telling the jealous girlfriend of Merlin that his former girlfriend—his so-called true love—had in fact loved him back?

Tobias nodded. His shoulders drooped. "I don't know what I was thinking..."

"And you wrote this to Gwen last month?"

Tobias shrugged. "Yes. But nothing came of it—I am sure. Gwen *can't* have passed on the information, for if she had, then surely Merlin *would have* written back to Millie."

Ella nodded, agreeing. What Tobias said made sense. And from Ella's own recollection of the day before, Millie had been upset and heartbroken. Dwelling on old wounds. She did not know that Merlin still harboured affection for her. Ella even recalled that Sally had said Merlin wouldn't even remember Millie!

Tobias looked up at the writers' walk archway. "After the accident yesterday and Millie's tragic passing... Though the past can't be undone, I decided Merlin deserved to know the truth. That Millie loved him and accepted his proposal all those years ago." Tobias shook his head, as if angry with himself. Regret etched his features. "I've been trying to muster up the courage all day and do just that." He regarded her with sad, pleading eyes. "Am I in the wrong?"

Ella held the schoolmaster's gaze. "What did Millie want? Did she tell you?"

"Millie planned to tell him," Tobias answered firmly. Voice full of conviction, he stood taller, as if bracing to hold his ground. "Before Sally talked her out of it. I know that much."

Ella folded her arms. It was not in her nature to meddle, but the truth needed to come out. Millie deserved to have her wishes upheld. The dead needed someone to speak for them. To reveal the truth. "Then you must respect Millie's wishes. Tell Merlin."

The relief on Tobias' face was palpable. He offered his arm. "Will you come with me? Merlin *has* to listen to me if you're there."

"You go on Master Tobias. I will follow along soon. There is someone I must talk to first."

Tobias looked surprised. "Who?"

Ella thinned her lips. "Sally."

CHAPTER 29

SALLY'S LAST CHANCE

NORTHGATE SQUARE, CHARMINGTON.

Who had the most to gain from Millie's death? Was her death by accident or design?

Ella pondered this question as she parted ways with the schoolmaster and trudged down the icy alleyway between the town hall and adjacent post office buildings. She paused on the corner of Mercer Lane, grateful for the last rays of sunlight as the setting sun streaked the mountain ridgeline with red and grey. Across the square, a flash of a buttercup-yellow pelisse and flutter of ostrich feathers bobbing on an ornate bonnet caught her eye over by the police station.

Sally? What was she doing?

The elderly haberdashery owner paused outside the police station. She ducked under a window sash so as not to be seen walking past by anyone inside and then cast a furtive glance over her shoulder before darting through the police stable gates.

Hmm...that was more than a little odd. Ella narrowed her eyes. What was going on here? Why on earth was Sally skulking around the back of the police station? In the many years Ella had known Sally, she had seen her stride, glide and go forth, but she had never seen her skulking... Something sinister was afoot, and, as usual, it looked like it was up to her to get to the bottom of it.

Steeling herself and drawing on her stoic resolve, Ella gripped her silver cane head and went to investigate.

MINUTES LATER, AFTER LIKEWISE CREEPING and sneaking her way in a very unladylike manner across the square and into the police courtyard, Ella stalked up behind Sally, who was jiggling the tack room door handle.

"Drat and blast!" Sally cried, releasing the handle and thumping her lace-gloved palm to the stout wooden door. "Locked! Now what will I do?"

Aware someone was behind her, the elderly woman started and clutched the yellow coat she wore over her black mourning silks to her throat. Her face was tear-streaked and on seeing Ella, she wailed, "Your Highness! What will I do? Please help me! I must extract the rogue's typewriter!"

Ella took a breath, her expression grim. "The typewriters aren't going anywhere, but I think you and I had better have a talk, don't you?"

Sally shut her eyes and gulped. Balling a sodden lace handkerchief to her face, at last she nodded.

They walked side by side, back across Northgate square in the twilight to the haberdashery. Sally uttered not a word, but she kept looking over her shoulder, squinting and staring at every face and stranger crossing the courtyard. Though the pair walked in silence, beyond the town wall, the clamorous sounds of the birds in the forest twittered and carried on in their preparation for nightfall.

Once Sally had closed the haberdashery back door and shut out the twilight and the noises of the evening birdsong, she pressed her back to the door. She sank down, pulling her bonnet from her head and mussing up her usually neatly arranged grey curls that now hung loose around her shoulders.

Ella fumbled through the darkened passageway, guiding Sally in her state of stupor to sit at the large cutting table, and then Ella set about finding a flint and striker to light several of the oil lamps and bring back a sense of warmth and security to the room. Soon soft light filled the haberdashery back room, illuminating the familiar shelves of silk hats, bolts of fabric and spools of ribbons.

Ella sat down beside Sally, looked deep into her reddened eyes, and said, "Whatever you have done. You can trust me. We are friends. More than that, I understand your pain..." With a sad knowing smile she said, "You see, a long time ago, the man I loved also did not love me back, but fell in love with my sister."

Sally burst into tears and clutched her face in her hands.

With a heavy heart, Ella let her friend cry, and she tutted to herself. Ah, Merlin, you old heartbreaker... But sometimes it was not intentional. She sighed. Just as Richard had not intended to break her heart, she knew Merlin had not intended to break Sally's. One could not knowingly break the heart of one that you didn't know harboured secret affection. Human hearts were the trickiest beasts of all creatures that dwelt in Wyld Enchantment Woods.

"Shall I make tea?" Ella said, as the town hall clock outside struck six.

Her words seemed to rouse Sally from her heartache. The other woman shook her head, lace hanky crushed in her fist. "There isn't time! You don't understand, I must fetch the typewriter! We are all in terrible danger!"

Ella placed a gentle hand on Sally's shoulder. "You had best explain. And then I will help you. You have my word."

Sally nodded. She took a deep, fortifying breath. "I knew Millie was meeting Merlin at eight a.m. yesterday to hand his *Red Riding Hood* novel draft back to him."

Ella arched an eyebrow, and before she could ask, Sally cut in, "Oh yes, I knew Merlin wrote *Cinderella*! We both knew! Millie thought she was the one he based the story on, you see! But it was *my* story—that night of the ball. I'm the one who lost a shoe on the steps when I was running after Merlin! That's how I knew he was the anonymous author, you see?" Sally held up a hand to cut herself off as if now wasn't the time for reliving old wounds.

"Is that why you typed those blackmail letters to Merlin?" Ella asked.

Sally's face drained white. "No! I did nothing of the sort!" she denied and jabbed a finger onto the tabletop. "But that note—the threatening one I told you about. Millie hadn't actually been receiving any threats—that was a lie. I told a lie. I admit it—the note wasn't sent to Millie! It was sent to me!" Sally gasped, and tears overcame her for a second. "I received it yesterday—a parcel was left out on the back veranda. After... after Millie...after Millie was crushed!" Sally clutched the hanky to her face. "I didn't find it at first, but when I did, it was just before Merlin came round last evening to offer his condolences."

Ella placed a soothing hand on the old woman's shoulder as Sally took deep breaths and struggled to carry on. "I was terrified! Afraid for my life, that I might be next. So I did as they instructed and stole the *Red* manuscript from Merlin. I swapped it for the fake they had supplied. And then I left the real *Red* manuscript under the writers' walk archway at midnight last night, as instructed."

Ella was surprised. "So this culprit, they *have* the *Red* manuscript?"

"I believe so." Sally gulped.

Ella turned the timeline of events over in her mind. Yesterday, Millie had delivered the fact-checked *Red* manuscript to Merlin at eight a.m. That's most likely what Marge the midwife had seen, the pair of them together. Then at nine a.m. Millie had been killed—struck by the falling typewriter when she had been walking under the archway, mere seconds after Merlin also passed that way. Then that night when Merlin visited Sally, she swapped the *Red* novel draft for the supplied fake. The fake that Ella and Merlin had discovered when his book satchel fell open while at the Huntsman tavern. So then, the culprit had the *Red* story, but the true author was very much alive... And Merlin had a second narrow escape today at the mayor's afternoon tea...

"And you have no inkling or suspicion who this person might be?" Ella asked.

"I have no idea who the rogue is! As I explained to Your Highness at midday, the instructions have always been typed! Until now. This came just before." She drew a crumpled piece of paper from her pelisse coat pocket and spread it flat upon the wooden table.

It was a badly handwritten letter—as if someone was writing with their other hand to disguise their handwriting.

> Fetch the small portable model typewriter labelled Hyde from the police tack room and wrap it and leave it on the edge of the unicorn fountain by half-past six.
> I will be watching.

Tears once more streamed down Sally's flushed cheeks. "But the tack room is locked—what will I do? The rogue killed Millie! Surely, if I don't do what they ask, they will hurt me! Or Olly! I can't take that chance! It's gone six now—I must get the tack room unlocked! I must beg that horrid Sheriff Axel for his aid!"

Just then, the door burst open and Olly and Tomcat tumbled into the room. On seeing Sally's distress, Olly flung themselves into Sally's arms and began soothing and offering all kinds of oaths to fix all her worries, while Tomcat bound up on the chair beside Ella.

As Olly consoled Sally, Ella regarded Tom's bright eyes and clean, shiny white coat. "You look so much better. Are you feeling better?" she asked.

"Much!" Tom's tail stood on end and his cat whiskers vibrated. "Goldilocks' healing magic has made me feel on top of the world! I feel like I've eaten a rainbow!"

"Really? That good, you say? Chalk one up to Goldi's exceptional prowess..." Ella blinked, and leaned back in her chair as beside her, Sally was assuring Olly that everything was going to be fine, and she wasn't upset because of anything that Olly had done or had had any more bad news.

Ella hummed to herself. No doubt the young orphan was feeling quite insecure and had had rather a turbulent time with sudden the traumatic death of their prospective adoptive aunt on top of the fact that their adoption process had not been finalised.

Ella felt a guilty start that she hadn't made a better impression on Mistress Fairweather, the orphan matron. Dear, oh dear, might she have to beg Merlin to sprinkle a little more of his charming fairy dust on the woman? No, that was hardly ethical. Not that she could understand what the ladies saw in her brother anyway and besides...

Ella suddenly realised the others were staring at her. "I'm sorry. I wasn't paying attention. What were you saying?"

"Rat in a box!" Sally beamed, and Tomcat bobbed up and down enthusiastically.

"Rat in a box!" Olly repeated, grinning ear to ear. "Me da used to use it all the time!"

Ella sat back. "Backup your thoughts a little more, my dear. I missed the conversation..."

Olly tugged the hem of their baggy black silk mourning frock and explained patiently, "It's a trick me da used to pull. When you ain't got the goods you is meant to deliver. You see, you just have to appear to be delivering something which looks about right from a distance—like a cute basket o' kittens, but on closer looksee, it's just a rat in a box."

As she struggled to comprehend the relevance of this dubious trick, Tomcat came to Ella's aid by adding, "Sally told us the rogue wants the typewriter, but there's no time to get it. But Olly says we don't need it anyway, Sally can just carry any old large box out to the fountain—"

"Rat in a box!" Olly chirped. "It don't matter what you give them— it only matters what they *think* they is getting!"

"—and then we wait and watch from the upstairs window to see who collects it." Tomcat tapped the side of his head. "Even though it's getting dark out, I will still be able to identify them with my cat's night vision!"

Ella stood up. "Excellent plan! With two slight alterations. One. Sally, you will loan me your distinctive yellow coat. I shall carry the box to the drop-off point—from a distance, you and I are indistinguishable, and I doubt they will be focused on whoever is holding the box, anyway."

"You are very kind, Your Highness." Sally touched her hand to her lips, gratitude welling in her eyes. "But I can't ask you to put yourself in danger!"

"Tosh!" Ella said. "This is my town! And Fortitude is my middle name."

Tomcat nodded. "And two? What's the second change?"

Ella grinned at Tom. "Cat in a box!"

ARE YOU OKAY?" Tomcat said from under the blanket and within the box which Ella carried across the dimly lit square toward the unicorn water feature. "Am I too heavy?"

"No, you're fine," Ella murmured, adjusting her grip. She kept her head down, her face partly obscured by the lapels and lace of Sally's buttercup-yellow coat Ella had borrowed. "The box is a little more bulky than I anticipated. And I admit, not having my stick, I am a little unsteady on my feet." But at least, Ella pondered as she shuffled across the expanse of Northgate square, if the rogue was watching her from the cover of one of the surrounding buildings, it would appear that she was labouring under the weight of something equal to the typewriter.

Unable to resist, she glanced at the few people who were out and about. Most, judging from their hurried manner and the hour just struck, must be on their way to family and meals awaiting them in the warm snug kitchens of their homes. There was Mr Beau, the shoeshine man and streetlamp lighter, across the way, his ladder at the base of the streetlamp of which he was atop now, setting flame to the gas lamp.

Ella grimaced to herself, once more reminded of her disastrous encounter with Mistress Fairweather. The matron was right. A petition to reinstate the fairy lights rather than rely on the dim light that the expensive gas lamps produced was a sound notion. She promised herself she would add that to her list of priorities for town improvements. The fairy lights required some level of magic, but even when Sibylla's ban on magic resumed, surely people wouldn't turn down the chance to have well-lit streets once more?

"Ugh!" As if to prove the fairy lights usefulness, Ella stumbled in the low light, kicking the toe of her boot against the lip of the fountain.

"Are you okay?" Tomcat cried as the box lurched.

"I'm fine. Keep your voice down," Ella whispered. "I'm about to set the box down. Remember, stay still. We don't want to ruin the illusion by your movement inside there."

"Okay," whispered Tomcat in return, and Ella lowered the box onto the edge of the water feature. She stood to stretch the kink in her back and looked at the rearing unicorn statue that was the central piece within the fountain.

Surely, if she was being watched, there was no way for the rogue to tell her apart from Sally at a distance. It wasn't as if she had to act as an older lady—she was an old lady and her aching bones reminded her daily!

Still, to help aid the 'rat in the box' illusion that Olly had so cleverly suggested, Ella extracted the handwritten note that Sally had received and regarded it once more, as if checking to see if she had meet all the rogue's demands, when in reality it was another prop to make the anonymous viewer believe she was Sally.

Ella unfolded the badly handwritten note. Her eyes darted to the instructions even though she had them memorised.

> Fetch the small portable model typewriter labelled Hyde from the police tack room and wrap it and leave it on the edge of the unicorn fountain by half past six.
> I will be watching.

Written in a hurry? Or deliberately scrawled to disguise their handwriting? Surely no person had handwriting this atrocious? It was barely legible!

From the town hall clock tower, the giant hands of the cluckoo clock clunked and shifted, and the chime rang out the half hour.

Half past six.

Ella paced back and forth beside the fountain, as if trying to decide what to do next. Indeed, the note hadn't said whether to stay with the box or leave it. Was the rogue intending to meet Sally or not?

She scanned the square, but it appeared quite empty.

"All right," she whispered, shaking her head and peering at the box, always conscious that she was probably being watched. "There's no sign of anyone. I think you're right, they will arrive once I—once Sally—leaves."

"I'll be okay," Tomcat whispered. "Stick to the plan. You go back to the haberdashery."

The note tucked back in her loaned coat pocket, Ella nodded, and cast one last glance up at the looming old clock tower.

A few minutes later, she had made her way back to the haberdashery and joined Sally and Olly on the second floor

"No one has approached the box," Olly hissed, not turning their gaze away from the window, where they covertly peeked between holes that Sally had cut in her fine damask drapes.

Sally kept peeking and then turning away. "Oh, it's so dreadful! That dear brave cat!" She pinched her brow. "My poor old eyes, I can't make anything out. Oh, dear, I'm no use!"

"Don't bump the curtain!" Olly warned and without shifting their gaze from the task at hand, Olly waved the fussing elderly stepmother back. "Me da used to say, there is some cut out for the game, and some who ain't."

Minutes ticked by.

Still, no one showed up.

Ella reflected on the meticulous planning of the whole thing. But what was so special about the typewriter they would risk exposing their identity to get it back? Was Merlin right? Had the owner's mind been so corrupted by the influence of black magic they couldn't part with it? And yet... And yet, they had the most important piece, surely? They had the *Red* manuscript. It was as if they were moving pieces on a chessboard, or directing players in a play. All chasing a clever lie...

"A lie... a lie... Someone has lied to us... Or, more to the truth of it, they have told us a lie and made us into actors in their play...." Ella slapped a hand to her face. "Of course! A lie! No one is coming for the typewriter—we've been played!"

Sally blinked. "Someone has played us?"

Ella nodded. "Yes! This has all been carefully planned." Ella grinned to herself. "All the world's a stage, and all the men and women are merely players. But call me fortune's fool, for I have overheard their exit strategy! Gretel said she had a special client! Leaving at six p.m.! Yes, it all makes sense now." She tapped Olly on the shoulder. "Quick, Olly, my dear, go fetch Tom. I must get to the auction house before the flying carpet sells! It's the only thing fast enough. We have a stagecoach to catch!"

CHAPTER 30

THE FLYING CARPET

Ella regarded the Sutherby auction house. The windows were all lit up against the fading daylight and the place rang with voices within its halls. The jaunty banner touting Grand Magical Auction Tonight 6pm onwards! was still strung across the entranceway of the old building, but from the number of people spilling out onto the steps, it appeared the auction must be over.

"Magic preserve!" Ella uttered to Tomcat at her feet. "Are we too late?"

"Let's hope not," Tom replied, darting across the street, his white fur reflecting off the glass of the doors as they entered the well-lit space filled with the hubbub of jovial people out for the evening.

Walking stick clasped in hand, Ella wove through those milling inside the grand auction house foyer and crossed the plush carpet. "There! Doctor Hyde!" Ella pointed out the doctor in his black duster who was standing near the auctioneer's podium and shaking hands with a foreigner dressed in long white robes. "Am I too late, Doctor? Has the carpet sold?"

"Ah! Mistress Charming! How lovely you look, yellow is a most becoming colour on you!" Hyde said, his usually dower expression split with a welcoming smile. He cast a glance at Tomcat at their feet and then gestured to the dark-haired man in white. "May I introduce Mr. Aladdin, he's the auction winner of your flying carpet." Judging from the enthusiasm of the doctor's greeting, the carpet must have fetched a hefty price.

"A thousand thanks." The foreign man bowed. "My master will be most pleased with the carpet—he sends me as his humble servant to collect such rare and priceless treasures as they come onto the market."

Ella squeezed out a smile in return and masked her disappointment. After all, the funds from the sale were going to a very important cause.

"Mr. Aladdin was asking after the history of the carpet," Doctor Hyde continued. "And I was just explaining I am merely the benefactor of the sale—the proceeds from the carpet going to restore the hospital roof—and that you are its proper owner."

"I confess I am not sure of its history other than my own short time as its owner." Ella smoothed her skirts. "The Sultan of Constantinople gave it to me, as a gift of thanks."

"Constantinople! I thought as much—the design, the quality!" Mr. Aladdin clasped the air as if confirming a suspicion. "Ah! Madam, you must indeed be a person of noble rank or magician of the highest repute for the sultan to part with such a treasure. Forgive this humble servant for being ignorant of your noble personage." He bowed low. "If you would please allow me a formal introduction so I might pass on my master's gratitude?" Mr. Aladdin bowed and reached for Ella's hand to kiss, his dark eyes twinkling.

"Assuredly, Mr. Aladdin, Ella Charming at your service—"

At her feet, Tomcat coughed and tugged on Ella's skirt, hissing, "Princess it up! Remember what Claude said! Lay it on thick."

Ella took the hint, unsubtle as it was. "Quite so. What I mean to say is, I am Lady Ella Discretion Fortitude Gertrude Charming. But the honour is all mine. Your master's gold from the purchase of the carpet will go towards funding the health of *my* subjects at the hands of our very competent Doctor Hyde." She nodded at the doctor, but Mr. Aladdin's attention was fixed solely on Tomcat.

"Did I just hear your cat talk?" The foreign gentleman blinked and stepped back. He regarded Ella with outright awe and bowed low. "Sell me the cat—my master will pay you double—*triple*—what we paid for the carpet! You have but to name your price!"

Ella and Doctor Hyde did a double take, from Mr. Aladdin to Tomcat.

"Hey! You can't buy me," Tomcat yowled, standing up on his hind legs. "I'm not for sale!" He tapped Ella's leg. "Tell him I'm not for sale!"

Mr. Aladdin gasped, his mouth formed an *Oh*, and he jumped back, his eyes cast down. "Forgive my impudence. A thousand apologies. I did not mean to overstep! But a talking cat! Never have I seen such a thing. My master would whip me should I not attempt to acquire him such a marvel!"

Ella blanched as other people's heads were turning their way. "I understand. No offence was taken." She smiled broadly and genuinely, adding, "Between me and you, it was the side effect of a magical spell gone wrong—not my finest achievement."

"Hey!" huffed Tomcat, crossing his arms. "I can hear you!"

Mr. Aladdin's smile returned, and he shrugged, nonplussed. "Is for the best. My master would not appreciate a talking cat that talks back!" He lowered his voice and added aside, "My master had a talking harp once—nightmare, let me tell you!"

They both chuckled, and Ella saw an opportunity. "If I may be so bold as to request a small favour—you see, Mr. Aladdin, I find myself in a rather desperate situation, and I need to get somewhere extremely quickly, if you follow my meaning."

Mr. Aladdin clapped his hands. "Ah! Of course! I shall be happy to assist. As fortune smiles upon me, I recently acquired a flying carpet!"

Ella played along, laughing and smiling. "They are extremely speedy, so I hear."

"Aren't they just?" Mr. Aladdin chuckled back. Then his expression changed ever so slightly and he held up a finger. "I must request one small favour in return. You see, my master plans to attend Prince John's coronation next year, and he wants everything to go smoothly for his grand entrance."

Ella's heart leapt into her throat. But she needn't have feared, as all he requested was for Ella to give his master a private demonstration on how to fly the carpet. "It wouldn't be for several months," Mr. Aladdin added.

"I can see no harm in that," Ella answered, looking for the clock at the back of the room. Gracious, they must hurry!

Mr. Aladdin stroked his beard and grinned at Tomcat. "Excellent. Excellent..."

Ella shook Mr. Aladdin's hand and then to Hyde said, "Goodnight, Doctor. Forgive my interruption to your evening. But now, I must fly! I have a stagecoach to catch!"

SOMETIME LATER, AS ELLA HUNG onto the flying carpet for dear life, the frosty wind chilled her bones and stung her eyes, reminding her why she had left the wretched square of carpet behind at the castle when she moved into her riverside cottage.

She lifted her head to shout, "Slow down!" To no avail. The wretched flying carpet had a mind of its own. On and on they sped. Fingers curled over the lip of the carpet, she pressed her cheek flat against the sandalwood scented red and gold woven fabric and closed her eyes.

"*Whheee!* Yeah!" Tomcat cheered at her side. Though likewise spread prone against the carpet as it zipped across the snow-shrouded treetops, Tom's cat claws and furry coat provided a more secure journey and an undoubtedly snug experience. "This is so much fun!" he shouted against the whistle of the wind, as his words were whipped from the air. "Can you make it go any faster?"

"No!" Ella shrieked, afraid the carpet might honour Tom's request. But all at once, the carpet swooped down, a sickening motion that left Ella's stomach twenty feet in the air while the rest of her tumbled off the carpet and rolled into a snowbank on the side of the mountain road.

"Magic preserve!" Ella sat up, spitting snow and wiping her face as the carpet, freed of the weight of its passengers, slowly spiralled back around and serenely glided to rest upon the frozen ground. Still and lifeless once more. Grumbling, Ella picked herself out of the snow and scanned the patch of the woods the carpet had off-loaded them in. "Tom?"

"I'm here, I'm okay," Tomcat said, bounding out the snow at the foot of a tall fir, and enthusiastically shaking snow free of his white coat. "Wow! That was awesome!" He stood on his hind legs and squinted left and right, up and down the roadside. "Where are we?"

"On the road to Avalon," Ella replied, bending down to roll the carpet up. Awkwardly, she lifted it on end so it might serve as something for her to lean against, but also to minimise the area of the carpet that touched the frozen ground. Should things go wrong, she didn't want to have to endure a soaking wet carpet ride home!

Tomcat darted back and forth across the road. "No tracks! We must be ahead of the stagecoach! You were right! The carpet was faster!"

Ella nodded. She patted the sagging roll of carpet. Though the ride had not been comfortable, it had certainly done the job. Now all they had to do was wait for Gretel's stagecoach and her mystery client and—

"Ella! Do you hear that? Horses! Gretel is coming! Get off the road. She won't see you in the dark!" Tomcat urged, paws tugging at the hem of Sally's yellow pelisse coat that Ella still wore.

"Have no fear. Even in pitch black, Gretel can see us," Ella dismissed Tom's concern as the thunderous clop of galloping hooves and jingle of harness heralded the stagecoach's approach along the bends of the mountain track. Through the trees, the flash of the lanterns darted like fireflies. "You forget what Gretel *is*. The coach's lanterns are for her customer's sake, not hers. Now, stand still. Gretel can see us very well, but we don't want to frighten the horses with sudden movement." She smoothed her hand across her windswept hair, hoping to cut an imposing figure rather than looking like someone who had just been dumped in a snowdrift.

All at once, the stagecoach drawn by four black horses rounded the bend and was upon them. Drawing up short, their hooves stomped the ground, nostrils flared as their horse's breath fanned the night air. Up on the box seat Gretel's yellow pigtails bobbed as she applied the brake and grumbled, "*Scheisse*! Is only you, Highness! I was hoping for a foolhardy robber. Is many years since a tasty snack landed in Gretel's path—stand and deliver!"

"My apologies for depriving you," Ella replied, leaning against the coil of carpet. "But I have to cut your trip to Avalon short." She squinted at the window glass. The shade was down, hiding the occupant. "You have a fugitive of justice aboard."

Gretel sighed and muttered something under her breath while Tomcat stood on his hind legs beside Ella and peered at the coach.

There was a flurry of movement within. The window blind lifted and light filled the glass, obscured as a figure leaned forward. Golden curls and a familiar dimpled smile appeared at the window glass.

Marge the midwife.

CHAPTER 31

THE FINAL SHOWDOWN

"Marge!" Tomcat yowled, white fur all spiky with surprise. "Marge is the villain? She killed Millie? Poisoned the mayor and stole Merlin's manuscript? I did not see that coming..."

With a grunt, Marge slid the sash open, leaned out the stagecoach window and pulled a sour face. "Oh dear, Lady Ella. I say this as a friend, but yellow is not your colour!"

Ella frowned at the yellow coat she still wore on loan from Sally and then cast a glance at the large stagecoach in the half light. The sun had set. Lanterns were positioned at every corner of the coach roof and Gretel herself was perched on the box seat and twirling a pigtail. Gretel lifted the reins and said, "Make quick talking, *ja*? Wheels freeze and get stuck in snow, I delay too long."

Ella nodded grimly. Marge was an unexpected fly in the ointment. Yes indeed, this whole affair had been planned and *plotted* so carefully...

Tomcat's tail flicked. He looked up at Ella. "I can't believe it's Marge."

"No, I can't. And I don't," Ella added, her breath puffed a cloud on the frosty night air. She took a moment to steel herself. Lies, secrets and jealousy. This all came down to one brilliant lie... "Show yourself!" she commanded. "I know you're in there, Tobias!"

A knife suddenly appeared at Marge's throat and from behind the midwife, a male voice said, "Beauty warned me this could happen." Tobias' pale face came into view. "I took precautions and brought a hostage."

"A hostage?" Marge's protest cut off suddenly as he pulled her back from the window.

"Ah. Master Tobias," Ella said, leaning on the rolled up flying carpet. "I guessed as much. When Millie came to you months ago, you learned of Merlin's secret identity as the author of *Cinderella*, didn't you? And that's when you and Beauty, as you call the typewriter, devised this plan to steal *Red Riding Hood* and publish it yourself."

Tobias smirked. "Then you know our plan is foolproof—"

He cut off whatever else he'd been about to say as Marge started complaining loudly about being brought here on false pretenses. "But *you* said this was a romantic getaway!"

Tomcat nudged Ella's knee. "What do you mean, you *guessed* as much? Why didn't you tell me?"

Ella shrugged down at the cat. "Who had the most to gain? Who needed the *Red* manuscript the most? It was obviously Tobias."

"But he's had one of his manuscripts accepted for publication—ah!" Tomcat slapped a paw to his head. "No, he hasn't! That was a lie."

Ella nodded. "Indeed. And a good one. No one would suspect Tobias as the thief of the *Red Riding Hood* manuscript if he *appeared* to have finally achieved success on his own." Ella now addressed Tobias, "Speaking of not doing things on your own. My compliments to your partner in crime. This has been extremely well planned. It's a shame you had to leave 'Beauty', the typewriter, behind. I have no doubt she was the true mastermind behind this dastardly scheme."

"And now you'll let me go!" Tobias said, the knife held to Marge's quivering throat. "Or Marge gets it!"

"Please! Lady Ella!" Marge wailed. "Please, do what he says! I'm not old like you! I've got so much to live for! Please let him go!"

"I fully intend to." Ella's smile was brittle, but her tone was calm and cheerful as she addressed the schoolmaster. "I just came to commend Tobias. After all, a clever plan is so much more satisfying when someone knows what you've got away with. A much better story to end on, wouldn't you agree?"

Tobias merely narrowed his eyes. In the dim light, the glow of the coach lamps revealed his pasty complexion had flushed despite his bravado.

Ella waved. "Bye, bye, now. Take care."

"What?" Tomcat huffed and sat back on his haunches. An indignant white form on the snow. "But you can't *really* let him take Marge?"

"She went of her own free will," Ella uttered with a nonchalant shrug, seemingly unconcerned. "Marge knew it was a getaway, of sorts, at least."

Tomcat crossed his paws tight across his tummy. "Ella, you can't be serious. She is clearly his hostage."

"But I find her quite annoying. Two birds, one stone."

"Ella!"

"Fine, fine, fine," Ella grumbled and held up her finger. "Second thoughts, Tobias. I've had a change of plans myself. If you release Marge unharmed, I will allow you safe passage. You come out of the carriage now and I will let you go. On foot." She grinned up at him from the dark of the snowy roadside, beaming widely as if they were simply negotiating the price of cheese. "You have my word, speaking as your beloved sovereign adjunct. Princess, princess, titles, titles. Agreed?"

"What do you mean, *you'll* let me go? On foot? *Ha!*" He brandished the knife and Marge shrieked. "See! I have the upper hand! I'm taking this coach all the way to Avalon! There's no way a lame old biddy is stopping me! Not even the queen herself could stop me!"

"You make a valid point," said Ella glumly, leaning a bit more heavily on the roll of carpet as it sagged in the fresh snow. And then, addressing Gretel, who was idly picking one of her fangs in the grey dusk and cupping her chin in her hand as if she were very bored, Ella said loudly, "Gretel, my dear, I rather think Tobias forgot to factor in his getaway plans, that the stagecoach driver is a vampire. Will you please dispatch Tobias for me?"

Up on the box seat, Gretel sat up from her slouch. "*Ja, ja.* But you pay for zee complete interior refit. Blood splatter ruins upholstery."

Tobias' eyes bulged. "Wait!" he yelled, pointing the dagger at Ella. "That other thing. The thing about on foot. We were discussing that!"

Ella half bowed. "As I was saying. You leave now, on foot. And how's this for generosity? You can keep the *Red Riding Hood* manuscript, too. Can't say fairer than that."

"But you can't let him keep the *Cinderella* sequel!" Tomcat yowled at her feet. "It's worth a fortune!"

"Tosh!" Ella rebutted with a dismissive gesture. "Merlin can just *write* another story. How hard can it be?"

From her perch on the driver's box seat, Gretel jangled the reins. "*Ja. Ja*, look. Ve have nice chit chat." Gretel's little white fangs glinted. "But back to zee business of Tobias for supper, *ja*?"

The carriage door suddenly swung open and Tobias scrambled out, his emerald cloak tangled around his legs, and he tumbled into the snow. On his feet and upright in seconds, he brandished the knife, swinging it right and left, between Gretel and Ella. Under his arm, he clutched a book satchel. "On your word, you let me go! Say it! Say it out loud! Don't let the vampire eat me!"

Ella rolled her eyes and looked heavenwards. "Upon my word, as right royal princess Ella, yada yada, Charming, official envoy, etcetera etcetera. You are free to go on foot."

"Boo!" Gretel shouted, outraged, standing up on the box seat and glowering down at Ella and at the frightened schoolmaster. Her lips drew back and she yelled at him, "Go zen, vat you vaiting for? Invitation? Go! *Run!*"

With a yelp, Tobias stumbled off along the snow-packed ground. Ella and Tom watched him until he disappeared between dark fir trees in the distance.

Grumbling to herself, Gretel snapped the reins, jostled the four horses and manoeuvred the carriage around on the narrow track. Marge's face slapped the glass with a bump. "Are you coming or not?" Gretel said, jumping down from the carriage box seat. She hoisted the limp magic carpet on top with an effortless flick of her wrist.

Marge's whimpering face pressed to the window and Ella exchanged a look with Tom. "Think I'll walk back. It's a lovely evening."

"Suit self." Gretel shrugged. She snapped the reins, and the stagecoach lurched and swayed, rolling away along the snow-rutted track back toward Charmington, with Gretel calling over her shoulder, "You owe me dinner!"

Ella began scouring the ground for a stick as Tomcat gestured to where Tobias had run off. "But Ella! Tobias killed two people. You can't let him go. Justice hasn't been served!"

Ella spied a suitable stick to use as a make-do walking stick and picked it up. "The chap is a writer. Writers aren't equipped to survive outdoors in the real world! He'll wander around and get lost." She pointed to the fir trees. "Did you not see? He even strayed from the path! It's embarrassing, really. His cursed Beauty was clearly the brains of their partnership. The chap could be outsmarted by a potato..."

The stick aiding her walking, Ella set off with Tomcat trotting at her feet. "And besides," she added, "as soon as we get back to Charmington, I'll send Wulf to track Tobias down. Justice will be served. You have my word."

CHAPTER 32

HOME AGAIN HOME AGAIN

RIVERSIDE COTTAGE, WYLD ENCHANTMENT WOODS.

"And then what happened?" Robinne asked as she scooped tea leaves into the waiting pot in the snug kitchen of Ella's riverside cottage, deep in the heart of Wyld Enchantment Woods.

Tomcat stood up on the scrubbed kitchen table. "And then Ella says, *'I can't. And I don't. Show yourself, Tobias!'* It was the coolest thing I have ever seen! It's such a shame you missed it." Tom turned to Ella, who was reading the classifieds section of the *Nottingham Times*. "One thing I don't understand. If Beauty was really telling him what to do, why would Tobias leave the typewriter behind? Surely it would have pained him a great deal to part with her?"

Ella tutted as she rocked back and forth in her rocking chair. "True love."

"True love?"

Ella nodded. "Tobias was a romance writer... think of all the novels he wrote on that typewriter. Maybe in the end, he taught Beauty a thing or two. Beauty's grand gesture was that she sacrificed herself for him. To help give him time to escape. It's as the saying goes, 'If you love something. Let it go.'"

"You think a *typewriter* sacrificed itself to help Tobias escape?" Robinne scoffed, placing the steaming mugs on the table.

"You would too if you'd been there!" Tomcat piped up. "We never would have caught the stagecoach in time if Ella hadn't worked it out. We waited and waited at the water fountain thinking he must turn up for the typewriter."

"Fine," the young woman said, hands on hips, "I might believe you if next time I'm there for the cool bit."

"Next time? What are you talking about?" Ella said, looking up from the newspaper. "It's not like we make a habit of this sort of thing."

"You solved Arthur's murder," Robinne said. "And Tom's the month before, although I guess that doesn't count? Since you're still alive?"

"Ella figured out Ace and the counterfeiting thing too," Tomcat added. "That was cool."

"Which, I might point out," Ella intoned primly, waving her pencil, "you *were* there for the *'cool'* bit."

"Oh yeah, I forgot about that one," Robinne said dismissively. "But anyway, promise me that next month I get to be involved with whatever mystery you two uncover."

"If you really want to be of use, then help me brainstorm some money-making schemes. If I don't raise quite a lot of money before Christmas, Sibylla is renting off land to build a prison, and I can't have that." Ella went back to scouring the newspaper for inspiration.

"Maybe we could put an advert in the paper and boost sales of Robinne's honey-bark cordial?" Tom suggested, turning to their young neighbour. "How much brew do you think we'd have to sell?"

"I'm guessing a lot more than the twenty something silvers I make a week," Robinne interjected with a glum sigh, glancing out at Ella's herb garden, as outside snowflakes fell.

"Unfortunately so," Ella mumbled, tracing a finger across the wanted adverts. "Doctor Hyde said the funds raised from the sale of the flying carpet will repair the hospital roof but only fund its running for six to nine months. So I can't imagine the three of us could *prepare* the volume of honey-bark cordial we'd have to sell to fundraise for an entire town."

"Perhaps," said Tom, tilting his head, "by the end of this amnesty month, because people will have enjoyed magic again, they will vote to have it reinstated? That would help restore the economy."

"Speaking of voting, have you heard that the mayor died?" Robinne drew a sharp, eager breath. "I was thinking, *I* could run for mayor! Charmington's youngest candidate! If I got the job, I could *easily* make people work together to improve the economy."

"One would think so... But the first rule of governance is, you can't reason with a mob. Save your heartache," Ella muttered. "There are easier ways to be entertained." She tapped a notice in the paper. "See here, Pickford Player's are holding open auditions next month. Play-acting being a ruler is much more fun—and a lot more peaceful."

Robinne leaned back. "I wonder which play Nigella will announce for her Christmas play?"

"Oh, I could audition!" Tom bounced on his seat. "That would be so much fun. I could act as a cat! That would be perfect!"

"Do they *have* any plays with cats in them?" Ella folded the paper down and looked over the edge. "I can't think of any? Can you two?"

From across the kitchen, Tom and Robinne returned blank stares.

"No. That's what I thought." Ella shook her head. Plays with cats in them. Ridiculous. She tapped her pencil against her lips and returned to the task at hand. "Anyway, at least it sounds like we'll have a very peaceful month ahead. Fortunately, play auditions and mayoral elections are unlikely to end in murder."

Tom's whiskers fanned out in a halo. "Unless the candidate's speeches *really* get out of hand! They say politics is cutthroat!"

"Hilarious, Tom, hilarious."

~THE END~

Next in Series...

Curse of the Scottish play or Charmington's first serial killer?

As the Charmington mayoral race begins, several candidates drop like flies.

Is it coincidence the theatre company is putting on the legendary cursed Scottish play, or is a bona fide serial killer on the loose?

The knives truly come out when the gentile arts face-off against the cutthroat world of politics.

Manners, motives and **black magic** wreaks havoc in

Death of Lady MacDeath

the next instalment in the Wyld Enchantment Woods mystery series.

Acknowledgements

Special Thanks to All Readers who take the time to Post a Review – I simply *cannot* continue without your support in sharing the word.

About the Author

Kura Jane Carpenter is a New Zealand author and was the 2019 recipient of the Sir Julius Vogel award for Best New Talent.

When not writing, Kura enjoys convincing strangers that greyhounds make the best pets.

Web: www.kuracarpenter.com

Instagram: @kura.carpenter

BookBub: https://www.bookbub.com/authors/kura-jane-carpenter

Goodreads: https://www.goodreads.com/author/show/22877105.Kura_Jane_Carpenter

Amazon Author Profile: https://www.amazon.com/stores/Kura-Jane-Carpenter/author/B0BGT43WSR

www.ingramcontent.com/pod-product-compliance
Lightning Source LLC
Chambersburg PA
CBHW021058130626
46552CB00005B/2160